DEAREST MILTON JAMES

N.R. WALKER

COPYRIGHT

Cover Artist: N.R. Walker & Sam York
Editor: Boho Edits
Publisher: BlueHeart Press
Dearest Milton James © 2021 N.R. Walker

All Rights Reserved:

Warning

Trademarks

Author's Note

All dates for conscription and references to defence force service are fictional. The author acknowledges there was no conscription for the dates mentioned herein.

BLURB

Malachi Keogh finds himself in a job he neither wanted nor asked for when his father, boss of Sydney's postal service, sends him to the end of the business line, aka The Dead Letter Office. Malachi expects tedious and boring but instead discovers a warehouse with a quirky bunch of misfit co-workers, including a stoic and nerdy boss, Julian Pollard.

Malachi's intrigued by Julian at first, and he soon learns there's more to the man than his boring clothes of beige, tan, and brown; a far cry from Malachi's hot pink, lilac, and electric blue. Where Julian is calm and ordered, Malachi is chaos personified, but despite their outward differences, there's an immediate chemistry between them that sends Malachi's head—and heart—into a spin.

To keep his father happy, Malachi needs to keep this job. He also needs to solve the mystery of the pile of old letters that sits in Julian's office and maybe get to the bottom of what makes Julian tick. Like everything that goes through the mail centre, only time will tell if Malachi has found his intended destination or if he'll find himself returned to sender.

Dearest Milton James

N.R. WALKER

CHAPTER ONE

YOU KNOW how there's one teeny piece of straw that supposedly breaks the camel's back? Well, I found it. And the invisible line one crosses with that one step too far? Yeah, well, apparently, I found that too.

Okay, so it probably wasn't just one piece of straw . . . Maybe it was a whole bale. And that 'invisible' line might have had approaching warning signs like exits on a freeway.

Whatever.

I sat in the backseat with my father as his driver escorted us from Sydney's head office of the postal service on Pitt Street to some warehouse of postal hell in the industrial suburb of Sydney's Alexandria. And if the arse-chewing I'd been getting at his office all morning wasn't bad enough, it continued in the car.

"You need to grow up, Malachi," my father said, not for the first time. "You're twenty-seven. You have no responsibility, no consequences. And that's my fault. As your father, I've let you get away with too much. Your brother and sister have shouldered . . ."

I tuned him out, and with a roll of my eyes, I stared out

the window. My very dear, very heterosexual brother and sister were the perfect children, quickly working their way up from the entry-level jobs, working hard, producing 2.5 grandchildren and picket fences in suburban houses with responsible mortgages.

Me, on the other hand, had just blown another job, went on a bender, spent a cosy night in a Kings Cross police station holding cell, and was released into the very responsible custody of my still pissed-off father.

Now, he didn't exactly not like the fact I was gay. He didn't love it, either. He also didn't love my black shaggy hair with a blue streak or my bright blue Doc Martens. Or the fact I'd paired a business shirt and tie with my faded black jeans with the knees out of them. He'd told me to dress respectably, so I did. It was my fancy tie and everything . . .

"Your mother insisted I give you one last chance," my father said. I'd almost forgotten he was talking. The incessant drone tended to fade away after several hours. "This *is* your last chance, Malachi."

I resisted sighing. Yes, getting my shit together was probably a good idea. But all those crap office jobs he'd insisted I take were not for me. Every time I tried to explain that, he refused to listen, spouting lines about 'not always getting what we want' yadda yadda, blah blah blah, and in the end, I just stopped trying to reason with him.

It wouldn't have mattered anyway.

We drove down the narrow, crowded back streets in Alexandria and pulled into the car park of some obscure warehouse. Actually, it didn't look obscure. It looked abandoned. It was old, dark brick with a saw-tooth roofline and windows for natural lighting, and there was a loading dock at one side. It had perhaps been an old factory or mill at some point.

It would make for a great nightclub.

Dad got out of the car and I reluctantly followed. "I've pulled some strings to get you this job," he reminded me. "Please don't disappoint me."

Ugh. The one d-word I didn't like.

We walked in through the door which led to a small entry hall. It was all decidedly beige: beige walls, beige lino flooring, beige seats. God, how miserable. Then we passed in through another set of double doors which opened out into the main part of the warehouse . . . and holy shit. It looked like the inside of a warehouse from a cross between an old war movie and an *X-Files* episode.

The place was bigger than it looked from the outside—I couldn't see the far end. The beige theme continued through to an office with glass partition walls and what looked like a tea room, though I couldn't see anyone around. There were some cubicle desks at the front, then rows and rows of huge shelves filled with boxes in all shapes and sizes. Along one wall were filing cabinets and those old catalogue drawers from libraries before computers were a thing. There were metal cage trolleys filled with more boxes and envelopes along the other side wall, and somewhere in the deep, tall rows of shelves, some kind of machinery beeped. A forklift, maybe?

So much beige.

"This way," my father said, walking toward the office. He knocked on the door and a man looked up, startled.

He was also beige. Well, not him, exactly. He was so pale I wondered if he was allergic to the sun. But his office, his desk, his hair, his glasses, his cardigan were all varying shades of brown. Christ on a freaking beige cracker. "Oh," he said, his voice deeper than I expected. He stood. "Mr Keogh. Please come in."

My father stepped into the office, unbuttoned his suit jacket, and sat opposite Mr Beige. I did the same, only because I didn't fancy getting far if I chose to make a run for it.

My father waved in my general direction. "This is Malachi Keogh," he said, his disappointment clear. "Malachi, this is Mr Julian Pollard, your new boss."

Beige Julian Pollard gave me a stern nod. "Nice to meet you."

I cracked a smile for him. "Likewise."

My father made a disappointed face. "Malachi has been told not to expect any special treatment. He is to behave responsibly like everyone else, and he will perform his duties as is expected of any employee. He can also be fired like anyone else."

I rolled my eyes, which Mr Beige saw. He didn't seem impressed, with me or my eye-roll, but I didn't care. He had a professor-teacher vibe going on which I could totally appreciate. I'd favourited a few of those porn videos on GayHub in my time. But it didn't matter. I wasn't going to be here long.

Whether he liked me or not was neither here nor there.

I felt like a kid at his parent/teacher night, getting the same old 'Malachi would achieve better grades if he stud-ied/talked less/did his work/turned up to class' kind of spiels. And I guessed in a lot of ways, that's exactly what this was.

My dad was literally taking me to my job interview . . . Well, technically it was my first day . . . of the job my father lined up for me.

I pretended I wasn't embarrassed.

Then I pretended I'd heard whatever it was they'd been talking about, which I most definitely had not. My father stood, rebuttoned his jacket, and gave Mr Beige a nod. "Thank you again. Malachi, I'll be back to pick you up after five."

Wait . . . what?

Five what?

"Five what?"

He didn't answer. He just turned on his heel and walked out.

"Five what? Minutes?" I called out after him, but it was too late. He was gone.

"I believe he meant five o'clock," Mr All-Brown replied.

Five o'clock . . .

There was a clock on the wall, which was somehow also beige, that indicated it was just after ten. "That's not on London time, by any chance, is it?"

Mr Taupe stood up, and he was absolutely wearing brown trousers and brown shoes. For the love of tan . . .

"I'll show you around and get you started," he said, turning his hand up toward the door.

Oh, hell no.

I was just about to bail, say thanks but no thanks, and take my chances with my father when Mr Beige looked up at the door and smiled. "Good timing. It's morning teatime. I'll introduce you to the team."

"Oh, you know what?" I tried. "That's okay. I don't think—"

"Mr Keogh was very clear," he replied, his deep voice pulling a thread at the bottom of my spine. He spoke with such authority and certainty, I was beginning to think he'd rattled some kink cage in my brain that found daddy-teachers hot.

Or him . . .

Was he hot? With his sensible hair, his brown glasses, brown cardigan—

A cardigan, Malachi. In no definition under any circumstances is that sexy.

Except it kinda was . . .

"Malachi?"

"Yes?" I answered too quickly.

He was standing at the door with one unimpressed eyebrow raised. "This way, please."

I stood and went with him to the staff breakroom. There were four people who all stopped and stared, coffee mugs in hand. And one by agonising one, I was introduced.

Paul, who I put at sixty-something, with his short grey hair, grey loafers, and a trucker's coat. He looked like Jeremy Irons . . . if Jeremy Irons ever starred in a movie as a trucker grandpa who delivered presents to sick kids at Christmas. Or maybe a trucker grandpa who murdered hitchhikers up the highway. Honestly, it could have gone either way.

Cherry was a goth girl, maybe twenty-five. She wore a purple plaid skirt over black tights, a black shirt, with a short black bob hairstyle, dark eyeliner, and dark lips. She looked me up and down, and after glaring at me, she gave me a nod. And everyone knows a nod from a goth girl is as good as it ever gets.

Theo was in his thirties, wore blue jeans, sneakers, and a polar fleece sweater vest over what I think was a football jersey? I didn't look too hard. It screamed hetero man who still lived with his parents, but he smiled wide and I immediately felt bad for judging him.

And Denise, a forty-something-year-old woman who wore KingGee work shorts, Timberland boots, a flannelette shirt with the sleeves rolled up. She had short blond hair, shaved up one side. She had tattoos on her forearms, and even though she looked small, I reckoned she'd be as strong as an ox and also a lot of fun to get on the piss with on a Friday night.

"This is Malachi," Mr Sexy Beige said. "He's replacing Glenda."

They all frowned and looked to a photo on the wall, which I quickly realised was a shrine. There was a memorial photo of an older lady stuck to the wall, like a plaque, but this was on purple funeral notice paper and stuck up with Blu-Tack next to the fire safety plan.

Nice.

Mr Taupe waited a respectful moment before continuing. "I'll be showing Malachi the ropes this morning. Then, Paul, he can work with you this afternoon."

Paul gave me a smile.

Oh goodie. The serial-killer truckie. How fun.

I waved. Not like Forrest Gump, more like one of those sun bears stuck in a zoo. Then because I felt like an idiot, I decided to open my mouth and prove that I was one. "I don't know how long I'll be here for. Until I disappoint my father again, no doubt, so probably not long. The odds are definitely not in my favour for that, let me tell ya. He's the boss of the postal service, just so you know. But please don't hold that against me."

Mr Boss McBrown hesitated. "I uh, um, I wasn't actually going to tell them that."

"Well, I'd prefer it put out there for everyone to know. So there's no surprises later on. I'm not a spy or anything. Cause trust me, he would not pick me for that. I believe the words my father used were 'childish disappointment' which, I mean, he's technically not wrong. But . . . anyway,

I'm getting off track. I'm sure everyone here is really nice, and RIP Glenda." I gestured toward the memorial photo, squinting at the details. "I'm sure anyone with five cats and an accordion was everyone's friend. I didn't realise I was replacing anyone, and this is not my choice to be here but more of a punishment for the whole 'wearing a skirt to work' and 'being arrested for drunk and disorderly.' I wasn't drunk at work, just so we're clear. And not that working here is a punishment at all; that sounds bad and I don't mean it in a bad way . . ." *Christ, Malachi, stop talking.* "But anyway, my point is that I probably won't be here for long, so feel free not to expend too much time or energy in training or getting to know me. It's honestly understandable, and that's it. I'm done talking forever now."

The five of them stared at me for a long few seconds.

Then Paul snorted out a laugh and sipped his coffee. Theo nodded to the kitchenette. "Find a coffee cup in the cupboard. Milk's in the fridge."

Cherry put her coffee cup to her lips, kept her head down, and sat at the table, facing the wall. And Denise barked out a smoker's laugh. "Love your boots. Did you get them from the Newtown store?"

"Uh . . ." I blinked. Did no one notice my verbal spewage just now?

Mr Tall and Taupe put his hand on my elbow. "You're going to want to wash any coffee cup you use first if it's been in the cupboard for a time. And remember to wash it afterwards."

I was still a little stunned. Either everyone here was used to a certain kind of crazy or I'd walked into an episode of the Twilight Zone. I was beginning to think it was the latter.

I chose a coffee mug from the back of the cupboard, that

was a ghastly shade of puce with an orange flower painted on it. Chances are it had been here since 1973 and the likelihood of someone using it any time in the last forty years were slim to none. I didn't even care that they all watched me wash it thoroughly, twice, before I used it.

After we'd finished our coffee, Mr Fawn and Fine began his tour of the warehouse. "So this is the Mail Redirection Centre. It used to be called The Dead Letter Office, but that sounded so . . . final. Anyway, we receive over two thousand undeliverable letters and parcels every day and we need to do our best to find out who the intended recipient was, or failing that, who the sender was and see it delivered."

"Sorry," I interrupted, confused. "Let me just explain something real quick about how this is going to go. I won't be staying."

Mr Beige smiled, his lips were pink, his brown eyes sparkled behind those brown frames. That gorgeous motherfucker smiled like he knew something I didn't. He smiled like this *was* the Twilight Zone and I'd entered the Hotel California and once you checked in, you could never leave.

He ignored my request to leave completely and waved his hand at one of the cubicles. "And this here is your desk."

CHAPTER TWO

"SO ALL THESE parcels and packages are just full of stuff people tried to send to someone?" I asked.

Mr Beige—I mean, Mr Pollard. I really had to stop calling him beigeful names in my head because they would undoubtedly start coming out my mouth. Mr Pollard was showing me through the warehouse.

He nodded. "Yes. Most we can reunite with its intended recipient, some with its sender. Takes some sleuthing, but that's what we do. We have about a seventy per cent success rate." He seemed very proud of this.

"Why does it go so awry?" I asked. "I mean, how do people get it so wrong?"

He paused at one shelf and plucked a random parcel. It was a brown box about the size of a shoebox, and there'd been some obvious water damage. He turned it over in his hands. "Label was ruined, the writing disappeared when it got wet. No return address."

"So it just sits here unopened forever?"

"No." He put the box back. "We open it to see if there is any ownership evidence."

"You open it? Isn't that some federal offence? You can't just open someone else's mail."

"Us and customs are the only agencies who don't require permission to open any mail."

I was a little surprised by this. "What kind of ownership evidence are you looking for?"

Mr Pollard shrugged. "Anything from letters, photographs, names on cards, telephone numbers, invoices, email addresses. Something that will give us an ID. That kind of thing."

I thought about that for a second. "Photographs? Like in the olden days?"

He chuckled. "You'd be surprised. Not all photos are digital. I know it's not easy for someone of your age to believe."

"I'm twenty-seven," I offered for absolutely no reason whatsoever. Probably because I looked sixteen.

"I know. Your father told me."

I made a face. "Did he? I tuned him out when he was talking, sorry."

"I could tell. And so could he."

I shrugged. "So how do you use photographs to identify and locate someone? Do you have face recognition software or something?" I looked around . . . There was no way this place had that kind of technology.

He chuckled. "Ah, no. But there might be photographs with names written on the back or a group staff photo with a company logo on it, who we can then call. Once, there was a school class photo from the 80s, amongst other things in the package. There was a handwritten note that said, 'Dear Joe, found the photo you wanted. Love Mum.' Looked at the photo with all the student names; there was only one Joseph.

And just like that, we had surname and a school and town."

"Uh, that's actually like police detective work."

That earned me a smile. "We call it detective work, unofficially, of course."

"That's pretty cool." I hated to admit that I was a little impressed. "What's the best thing you've ever found?"

"Jewellery, expensive artwork, war medals. A surprising amount of antiques."

"Anything gross? Like severed fingers?"

He eyed me oddly. "Uh, no." Then he shrugged. "We do see some live animals from time to time."

Now it was my turn to be horrified. "In the post?"

He nodded, then sighed. "Usually small critters like lizards and turtles on their way to overseas somewhere. Though most of our work is very mundane, it's still very rewarding when we can deliver something once thought lost."

"What happens to the stuff that can't be returned?"

"Depends what it is. If it's valuable, like jewellery or cash, it stays here for a year. If it's just letters or cards or clothes, maybe three months. Then it all goes to government auction."

"You sell it?"

He nodded. "The government does, yes. Everything from gift cards to Gucci shoes, PlayStation consoles to power tools. You name it."

Wow.

He showed me the loading dock, the huge metal trolley cages that were filled with parcels and letters that we were supposed to process. Then he showed me how to use the digital scanner thing and how the computer software worked. Then he had me take a few mail items and enter them into the system.

Everyone else just did their own thing. Theo wheeled his cage trolley down the aisles of alphabetised packages, then came back with something, scanned it, typed on his computer for a bit, then hurried back down the aisle.

Cherry sat at her desk, opened some letters, and searched up some address on Google Maps. She squinted at the screen a lot, kept her head down mostly, went wandering off down the aisles, and came back with her nose in a different set of papers.

Denise was the one on the beeping machine, which turned out to be a cherry picker for reaching the top shelves. "Aerial work platform," Mr Pollard corrected me. "Denise is also a licensed forklift driver, so if you need anything moved or retrieved from the top shelves, give her a holler."

I didn't see much of Paul . . . I heard whistling coming from the dark depths of aisle J-K-L and I assumed it was him.

But everyone kept very busy. Piles of letters, parcels, packages, even luggage. Who the hell sent luggage in the post?

I even did some parcels from overseas with barcodes that were surprisingly easy to track down. Well, easy as putting a submission form to the UK postal service portal with the barcode details, and through the magic of the internet, sender and recipient information was retrieved.

Theo took a phone call from someone who was looking for a birthday gift from China that never arrived. They had a serial number, so Mr Pollard had me look it up and, lo and behold, it was being held in aisle S. I took my little scanner thingy down to that section and matched the barcode.

"Is that it?" I asked excitedly.

Mr Pollard pulled the box out, double-checked the scanner, and smiled. "We have a match."

Oh my god. We had a match.

"We have a match!" I echoed, far too excited for this stupid job I was forced to do.

Theo confirmed the recipient's proper address. We labelled it correctly and put it back into the system.

How on earth was it that exciting and rewarding to send someone their mail? I had no clue, but it was. And I even tried to tamp down my enthusiasm. "Can I do another one?" I asked.

Mr Pollard smiled. "You can do hundreds."

"Oh."

Well, one was exciting . . . a hundred sounded a lot like work. But I did another letter. The front was marked *Not at this address* and there was no return address. Inside was a beauty company's promotional discount voucher. It was a mass-produced marketing thing and it was a dead end. It went into the bin marked for shredding.

Not as exciting as the first one, but still.

Soon enough it was lunchtime, for which I had to raid the vending machine because I'd arrived here this morning with nothing but my father and a shitty attitude.

Everyone seemed nice, bar Paul. I mean, he did offer to share his lunch with me. Which was kind and generous, I'll admit. But I'd seen those episodes on the crime channel where serial killers have bodies in their freezers, and Paul's lunch looked decidedly suspicious.

"It's vegan," Paul said, still trying to convince me to eat half his food. "Plant-based pork."

Plant-based pork . . .

"No thanks, but I'm interested to know which plant they use for that. Like what actual plant goes into plant-based food. Is it a general garden variety? And why don't they specify?"

"I think it's soy," Paul replied. He read the label. "Textured soy protein."

I tried not to grimace. "Sounds delicious. But I'm good, thanks." I held up my vending machine packet of sodium and saturated fats disguised as potato crisps and realised his lunch actually sounded better than mine. "I'll remember to bring something tomorrow."

Tomorrow . . .

Would I even be here tomorrow?

"Anyway," Paul said, his thin lips in a sly smile. "Hurry up and finish your plant-based lunch. We got a lot to get done this arvo."

A trucker serial killer with a feisty sense of humour. I liked it. My lunch was indeed also plant-based. I chuckled. "Touché."

And so, for the next few hours, Paul showed me how he did things. His tips were to wear just one earbud to listen to your favourite 'jams'—his word, not mine, dear god—and still hear what's going on in the warehouse. Wear a coat in winter or you'll freeze to death. "Label everything that goes into the fridge, though the food stealing has stopped since Glenda died, so draw your own conclusions with that," he said.

"How did Glenda die?" I asked as we packed new parcels away on aisle T-U. "She looked nice in the photo on the wall. Strong too, to hold an accordion that big. And all those cats . . ."

Paul almost smiled. "No one knows. She didn't turn up for work one Monday. Julian tried calling but no answer, so he called the cops to do a welfare check. Turns out she'd died on the Friday before."

"Oh, that's terrible."

"They found her in her chair. Rumour has it the cats ate her fingers. Can't open the tins of cat food, ya see, so the critters gotta eat something."

Aaaaaand just when I was starting to think he wasn't a serial killer.

I tried to play it cool. "Guess there's a lesson in that for everyone."

He stopped pushing the cage. "Guess there is."

He took down a box from the shelf and added a letter to it, scanned the letter and the box, and entered in the date and code so we could find it should anyone ever claim it.

"So what's Mr Pollard's story?" I asked, ever so smoothly.

"Mr Pollard?"

Mr Brown. Mr Sexy Beige. "Uh, Julian."

"Oh, he's okay. Keeps to himself mostly. Lets us do our thing. As long as the work's done, he doesn't care."

"He wears a lot of brown."

Paul snorted. "Never seen him wear any other colour. Not like you. With your peacock hair and matching boots."

I looked down at my Doc Martens. "These are called Colour Pop blue. And my hair is ninety per cent black. The matching blue streak is called Bad Boy blue."

"Do all the girls like it?"

"I wouldn't know. The boys do though." I just threw that out there. I'd never been shy about my gayness. "And when I get sick of the blue, I just bleach the strip of blue out and change colour. Last one was pink. I have the matching boots for that as well."

Paul met my eyes and smiled. "Trendy. Back when I

DEAREST MILTON JAMES   17

was your age, all the rage for guys was long mullets and moustaches."

"Nice. Love a good porn 'stache."

He laughed and kept pushing his cage, slowly filing away all the undelivered parcels. I had to jog a little to catch up. "So, what's the weirdest thing you've ever found in a parcel?"

"A box full of dildos."

I snorted. "Nice."

"Used."

"Gross." I shuddered. "Is there anything that lives in infamy? Something that still gets talked about? Or even better, something that no one talks about? Like you all just pretend never happened?"

"We get weird things all the time. Like false teeth, wooden legs, a whole range of sex toys, you name it." He shrugged. "Nothing we don't really talk about because it's gross. But there is that pile of letters in Julian's office that we don't really talk about."

"What letters?"

He sighed and pushed his cage to the next stop. "A pile of letters from the 1960s or 70s, I think. I dunno what's in them. They were here long before me. Found 'em all bundled up in the back of a pigeonhole; must've got lost a long time ago. But he read 'em, Julian did. And he tried to find the owner." He slid a box onto the shelf and did the scanner thing. The machine beeped and he looked at me. "Couldn't tell ya what's in them letters. Only that they're all addressed to the same man, no address at all. Like he was writing to Santa Claus or Jesus or something." He rolled his eyes. "We get a lot of those too."

He had my undivided attention. This had intrigue written all over it. Not just the letters, but why Mr Sexy

Taupe kept them after all this time. "What's the name? On the letters, who are they all addressed to?"

He frowned as he tried to recollect. "Um . . . dunno. Oh." He tapped his finger on the cart. "That's it. They're all labelled to a Dearest Milton James."

CHAPTER THREE

"I TRUST YOU WERE WELL BEHAVED," my father said in the car. We were both in the backseat again, his driver pretending he couldn't hear anything. And true to my father's word, he picked me up at five o'clock. Honestly, I think he was surprised to see me still there. He must have assumed I'd bailed hours ago.

"Yes, of course I was."

"You even seem . . . happy."

"Would you prefer me to be miserable?"

"No. I just wasn't expecting you to be smiling when I picked you up."

"You weren't expecting me to be here when you picked me up."

My father did that eyebrow thing where his left one would twitch upward, and his lips were kinda pursed. It was his sarcastic face that basically said, 'no shit, Sherlock,' without him having to say it.

"So you'll be going tomorrow," he said. It wasn't a question. It was a statement. Or an order.

"You know what?" I asked.

He looked at me.

"I think I might." I smiled. "I actually liked it. I don't know if I'll like it tomorrow or in a week from now, but today was fun."

"Fun?"

"Yep. It's not a boring desk job and I don't have to deal with arsehole customers. Or even the nice ones. There are actually no customers. Except the odd phone call. But no interaction with the general public at all. That's the selling point right there."

I was never cut out for a boring old desk job. Or dealing with people. I'd told him this a hundred times but he'd never listened.

"And we get to do detective work," I added. "We get to look in envelopes and packages and try and figure out who the intended person was. I'm like a real-life Sherlock Holmes."

My father stared at me, probably trying to gauge if I was being sarcastic or not. "So you . . . you actually like it?"

I shrugged, aiming for indifference. "I liked it today. And that's more than most other jobs I've had."

He did that eyebrow thing again, this time with more surprise. "Well, I'm glad to hear that."

"I don't know how long I'll like it for, so don't get too excited."

"But you're going tomorrow?" It was definitely a question now.

I smiled. "I think I will, yes." The car pulled up out the front of my block of flats in Newtown. "No need to chauffeur me tomorrow," I said. "I can bus it."

This surprised my father too, but I closed the door with a cheerful flourish and a wave and went straight up to my one-bedroom flat. It was very small, very old, somewhat

dank and dreary—and yet still ridiculously expensive to rent
—but it was mine.

My own little piece of independence. Everything in it
was mine: the mismatched furniture from op-shops, the
vintage glassware and the retro plates, the old vinyl albums
from a second-hand bookstore that were now on the wall as
artwork.

It was all mine.

And yes, the bills were mine too. And the rent I had
to pay.

But in the five years I'd lived here, I'd never missed a
payment. Despite my inability to find or keep a job that
held my attention, I'd always managed to scrape by.

My parents rode a constant tide of disappointment and
dismay when it came to me. Probably as much as they disappointed me. We had a strange relationship; they had forever
set bars of expectations and I'd forever fallen short, yet they
admired my grit and the tenacity with which I stood my
ground. Traits gifted to me by my mother and father respec-
tively. And I respected their morals and ethics on the politics and open-mindedness for change.

I wasn't particularly close to my brother and sister.
They were a bit older than me. But all in all, there was a lot
of love in our family. We just drove each other crazy to even
the balance of the seesaw.

I guessed most families were the same.

After an inspection of my very empty fridge, I made a
trip to the supermarket. I grabbed a few things for dinner
and also some stuff for lunch for the week. I was almost
excited to be buying lunch stuff because I was excited about
going to work, which was ridiculous.

I was certain the bubble would burst, possibly as early
as tomorrow. I could walk in there tomorrow and Mr Beige

and Secretly Sexy could decide I wasn't a fit for his team and he could fire me.

Even though his team were a bunch of misfits and I'd probably never fit in anywhere more . . .

Anyhoo . . .

I arrived to work the next morning a little early—I certainly didn't want to be late—but it seemed that everybody did the same. Everyone was in the staff room having their first coffee, talking about their mornings.

"Hey, Malachi," Denise said, bleary-eyed but cheerful.

"Morning," Theo said brightly.

"Nice sweater," Cherry said from over her steaming coffee cup.

I looked down to my pink argyle knitted sweater, then grinned at her. "Thanks. I have a sunshine-yellow one and an apple-green one as well, but I was totally feeling the bubble-gum, pretty-in-pink look today."

That was me. When a simple *thanks* would have sufficed, I had to open thine mouth and allow the word vomit to pour forth.

And because I wasn't quite done, I stuck out one foot to show off my very pink Converse boots. "And of course I have to match."

"Do you have shoes to match every colour?" Paul asked. He was sitting at the table, coffee in one hand, newspaper in the other. I couldn't decide if his question was sarcastic or not, so I chose to believe it wasn't.

"Generally speaking, yes. Or if not, I add an accessory to bring the whole look together." Then because there was a chance he was being sarcastic, I added, "Only three things in this world can pull off the matching colour look. Gay people, Power Rangers, and Teletubbies. And when I say pull off, I mean—"

Someone cleared their throat by the door. "Good morning."

Mr Pollard was pointing a rather stern look in my direction, as if he was well-aware of what I'd been about to say.

He was wearing all brown again: taupe trousers, a fawn shirt and a brown cardigan with brown double stitching and oversized brown buttons.

Was there a brown Power Ranger? I couldn't remember. But there was definitely no brown Teletubby. And if he wasn't a Teletubby or a Power Ranger, then oh my god, he had to be . . . Holy shit, was he gay?

My internal-me was banging on the side of my gaydar because there seemed to have been a glitch.

Surely not.

Could he be?

I mean, he was hot . . . in a sexy professor kind of way. His short brown hair, pink lips, and his brown glasses, those killer brown eyes . . . and not killer eyes like Paul the serial killer, but killer eyes as in 'if he aimed that stern glare at me again, I might die' kind of killer eyes.

He had a quiet confidence about him that I was attracted to. But the brown . . .

Such an odd choice.

"Morning," I said somewhat too late. I must have been standing there having my gay epiphany for too long. So I quickly made myself a coffee and tried to disappear.

"Uh, Malachi, can I see you for a minute?" Mr Sexy Professor asked. "When you've had your coffee. No rush." He took his coffee and disappeared into his office.

I frowned. "Is that a good 'can I see you' or a bad 'can I see you'?"

Denise scoffed. "Is there ever a good 'can I see you' when it comes from your boss?"

Oh no . . .

"What did I do?" I asked.

"I don't know," Paul said with a smirk. "What *did* you do?"

"Nothing. I don't think." I tried to wrack my brain. "I was early and I brought my own lunch." Then something occurred to me . . . I gasped, hand to my offended little heart. "Am I too gay? Should I tone it down? Is the pink a bit too much? I was going to wear fuchsia suspenders over a My Little Pony shirt but decided that might be too much gay for day two."

Denise put her hand on my arm. "Calm down. Do I look too gay?"

I looked her up and down. "Not at all. Name one lesbian lumberjack that isn't gay enough."

Theo choked on his coffee.

"Exactly." Denise grinned. "Wear what you want, be who you want. Our only policy here is that you be nice, you clean up after yourself, and bring cake for birthdays. That's it."

I nodded. "I like cake."

"Believe me," she murmured, "Pollard has no issue with us gays." She finished with a wink and walked out.

Right, then.

So Pollard was gay?

I downed half my now-tepid coffee while I tried not to think about what Pollard might want with me and decided to go in and find out. I quickly washed and dried my cup and knocked on his open door. "You wanted to see me?"

"Oh yes, take a seat." He rifled through some papers on his desk and put a form in front of me. "Just some paperwork we didn't cover yesterday."

"Oh." My relief was instant. "I thought I'd done something wrong."

He half-smiled. "How was your first day yesterday?"

"Good. I think. I enjoyed it."

"I'll put you with Cherry this morning. She can run you through some more basics."

Oh. "Uh, just between you and me, do you think I might talk too much for her?"

He smiled properly this time, his eyes warm. "No. I think you'll get along just fine. She's very good at searching online for obscure clues."

"Oooh, obscure clues. That's exciting." I realised I was clutching the form he wanted me to fill out. "Uh, do you have a pen I could use?"

He took one of three pens that were neatly organised in a line under his computer monitor and handed it to me. I began to fill out the tedious government workplace safety form, hoping I wasn't taking up too much of his time. I realised then that he was watching me write. "Sorry, do you want me to take this somewhere else?"

He shook his head slowly. "Not at all." He seemed embarrassed. "Uh, yesterday you mentioned getting fired for being drunk and there was something about a skirt. Is that something we should discuss?" Then he baulked. "Oh, the drinking I mean. Not the skirt."

"I wasn't drinking or drunk at work. I would never do that. I got drunk after I was fired."

"And why were you fired?" he pressed. "I know I should be privy to this information before you were hired, but your father asked if we still had a position going and I don't question my bosses' boss."

I frowned. "I kinda feel bad that my father made you give me this job. You must think I'm a spoilt kid whose daddy fixes all his problems, and that's not exactly right." I cringed. It wasn't exactly wrong either . . . I took a deep breath. "I was fired because I wore a mini skirt to work. And you know, it wasn't even really the skirt, it was my attitude about the skirt . . ."

"And this was at a post office?"

"The administration head office, yes. You see, there's a uniform rule that states a woman's skirt can't be higher than ten centimetres above the knee. A girl I worked with got an official reprimand, which is a whole lot of bullshit, just between you and me. It was a standard-issue skirt purchased through the company. She shouldn't be penalised just because she's tall. But the whole thing reeked of a bigger issue."

"I think I can see where this is going."

I nodded. "Right? So to prove my point, the next day I wore a very short mini skirt. When the office manager called me in, with his eye twitching and his high blood pressure veins popping, I asked him to show me where in the holy guidebook it said that a man's skirt can't be that short or where it said that a man can't wear a skirt, and he started to froth at the mouth." I shrugged. "The drinking happened after he'd fired me, and I had a whole day free now, right? And I'd shaved my legs for the skirt. And I looked good in those heels. Not gonna lie. I was looking hot. I wasn't gonna waste all that effort. So I went to Stonewall and had a few too many drinks for far too many hours, and anyway, to cut a long story short, some guy had tried to solicit my services and I tried to give him a lesson in manners with my stiletto, so the police took me back to the station for a chat. That man was very rude and no one should treat sex workers that way." I put my hand to my chest. "Not that I'm a sex worker, but that doesn't mean I can't stick up for them. Same with the uniform and the skirt issue."

"So you were fired for . . ."

"Speaking up about gender equity and dress codes in the workplace. And, I'll have you know," I added proudly, "my father is having the dress code reviewed. So I'd call that a win."

Mr Brown and Smiling seemed to find something amusing. "Your father never mentioned any of that."

I snorted. "Uh, no. He picked me up from Kings Cross police station. To say he was not impressed would be a gross, gross understatement. And it was rude as hell, because believe me, the fact I could still walk in those heels after twelve hours drinking should impress everyone."

He sipped his coffee with smiling lips. "Agreed."

"Oh, the form," I said, getting back to the task at hand. "Sorry, I get side-tracked. And I talk a lot when I'm nervous."

"I've noticed."

"I thought I was in trouble."

"What for?"

"I didn't know."

He studied me for a long moment, searching for what I could only guess. In the end he smiled. "You're not in trouble."

Christ. Did his voice just drop an octave?

If we were out at a bar or something, I'd read that voice, paired with that look, as attraction.

But surely not.

Surely.

It was suddenly a few degrees warmer in his office, and I nervously looked around the room to find something to change the subject to . . . and that's when I saw them. Over his shoulder on a shelf.

The pile of letters.

They were old, yellowed by time, bound with twine. They stood on a small wooden platform like they were a trophy. "Can I ask about the letters?"

He cocked his head. "Which letters?"

"Those." I glanced pointedly at them. He followed my line of sight, turning side-on, giving me a wonderful view of his neck and sexy ear.

When the fuck had ears become sexy? *Get a grip, Malachi.*

I was in so much trouble.

"Oh," he said quietly. A fond but sad smile tugged at his lips. "Those are . . . those were here when I began working here. They have a bit of a story to them, and I never could bring myself to have them destroyed."

"Destroyed?"

"They're almost fifty years old. We don't keep lost mail that long."

"But you kept those."

He met my gaze and conceded a small nod. "Yes."

"What's the story? You said they have a bit of a story . . ."

Just then his desk phone rang and he looked up at the clock on the wall. It was 9:10am. "Oh." He straightened in his chair. "You should get to work. Go find Cherry. I'll need that paperwork done by the end of the day though."

I nodded, the sound of the ringing phone urging me out the door. I heard him answer as I left, "Julian Pollard speaking."

The sound of his deep voice saying his own name shouldn't have made me shiver, but it sure did.

"Oh, if you're cold, there's some old coats in the lost and found," Theo offered brightly as he pushed his cart along.

"I'll be fine," I replied. "Just need to get busy."

"Everything went okay in there?" he asked, gesturing to the office door. "You weren't in trouble?"

I held the form like a shield. "Nah, just forgot to fill in a form."

He gave me a smile with far too many teeth. "Always paperwork."

"Always." I looked around. "Seen Cherry? I'm with her today, apparently."

"Think she was in the Beetle aisle."

"The what?"

"The V-W aisle," he said with a laugh. "You know, the car? I always call it the beetle aisle. No one else does."

"Oh. Cool. Yeah, vee-dub. I get it. That's funny." It was not funny.

I put the form on my desk and went in search of Cherry. I did, in fact, find her in the V-W aisle. She startled when I waved. "Hey. Oh sorry, didn't mean to sneak up on you. I'm with you today, apparently. Mr Pollard said that I should find you."

"Mr who?"

"Mr Pollard?"

"Oh, Julian?"

"Yes, Julian. Feel kinda weird calling him that. Like calling your teacher by their first name."

Cherry almost smiled. She was wearing black and purple again today. Her severe black bob and dark purple lips matched her outfit perfectly. She reminded me of those Bratz dolls that were cool when I was little, and I loved that.

"I promise not to talk you to death," I said. "Julian said you were the best at searching online for obscure clues."

She shrugged. "Not really. Just good with Google, and I think outside the box."

"That's awesome."

"Here," she said, passing me a box from her trolley.

And we put a few parcels and letters on the shelves, cataloguing as we went. I even managed not to speak for a bit, which was some kind of record for me. But soon the silence became too much and I panicked that it was becoming awkward. "So how long have you worked here?" I asked.

"Three years."

"You like it?"

She nodded. "Love it. Get left alone, don't have to speak to anyone." Then she added, somewhat reluctantly. "And reuniting people with their stuff is pretty cool."

"It is." I scanned a small brown box and shelved it. "So, what's Julian's story?"

I tried to be casual but I was certain she saw through me.

"Why?"

I shrugged. "Dunno. Just curious. He seems kinda cool but he wears a lot of brown, and that's a fascinating choice to me. There's a story there, for sure."

"He's always worn clothes' like that. But I've always worn clothes like this, so . . ."

"And I've always worn clothes like this," I amended. I didn't mean to offend her. "But that's my point. It's an expression of identity or our mood or we just like it. So either way, I have to say that all that brown and beige is a bold choice."

She seemed to consider this for a while, opting for more silence, and I figured I wouldn't push my luck. But then she said, "He went through a pretty bad breakup, apparently, just when I started. So, like three years ago? He took it pretty hard. His boyfriend left him for another guy."

My brain pulled on the handbrake, sending me spinning to an abrupt halt.

Boyfriend?

"Pollard has no issue with us gays," Denise had said.

He *was* gay.

Well, gay, bi, pan, whatever . . . The point was, he liked guys.

My heart did a little double-beat for a second.

"Oh," I replied when I realised I hadn't said anything. "That must have sucked for him."

"Mm," Cherry replied, sliding the last box into place on the shelf. "Back to the front we go."

"Can you show me how you search for stuff?" I asked. "And all those obscure clues. It's the exciting part."

She nodded. "It's my favourite part."

I resisted the urge to do an excited jumpy-clap. Instead I smiled at her. "Mine too!"

The first few parcels were straightforward. One had an incorrect postcode, and the town name was spelt wrong. That was an easy fix. One parcel lost its address sticker but had a barcode from Tasmania, and a few phone calls soon saw that one on its way. One letter was marked *Not At This Address* and upon opening it, we found another mass marketing brochure and it went into the to-be-destroyed pile.

The next few parcels were from stores sending out online purchases. Labels were incorrect, torn, wet, missing. But inside were invoice copies with names, addresses, emails, and phone numbers. And these weren't just a cheap shirt from Kmart. Some of these were Fendi shoes, a brand-new iPhone, a Kitchen Aid, and other mind-boggling stuff.

"Oh yeah, this is what we see every day," Cherry said. "Train sets, vintage wines, Xboxes, mostly clothes."

So much stuff was bought online and sent through the postal system. There were a lot of eBay packages with labels in foreign languages. Whoever invented the barcode tracking system deserved a freaking raise.

We got most of them back in the system off to their rightful owners, which was amazing.

But then there was one envelope with a handwritten name and address. It looked like it might have been a birthday card, and it was clearly written by an older hand.

"What's wrong with this one?" I asked.

Cherry pointed out the very obvious. "No postage." She carefully opened it, and yeah, it was a birthday card with a message and a ten-dollar note.

The writing was chicken-scratch and wobbly, but it was sweet, and the thought of this little grandma's letter not getting to her granddaughter made me sad. Ten dollars would have meant a lot to either of them, I was sure. It was signed off, *Love, Nan*.

"Can we just send it anyway?" I asked. "I'm sure this sweet little old nan just forgot to put a stamp on it. Or maybe it came unstuck."

I got the impression Cherry wanted to roll her eyes and call me naïve, but she took pity on me for being new, I guessed. "We send the letter with a notification of non-payment."

I was horrified. "You're going to send little eight-year-old Elsa a bill? For a one-dollar stamp?"

"Plus an administration fee."

I gasped. "We're monsters." I picked up the card and slid it back into the envelope. "Can I pay for it? It's just a dollar. Surely we have stamps here that I can buy."

Cherry stared at me like I'd lost my mind. "To be honest, I'm not sure. I don't think anyone's ever asked. I mean, it sucks for Elsa and her nan, but if we do it for this one, we need to do it for all of the letters that come in like this. And we get a lot without postage every week."

I frowned. "We don't have to do it for all the letters that have no stamp. Just the ones from sweet old grandmas."

Cherry shrugged. "Might wanna check with Julian first."

I glanced over at his office door. *No time like now* . . . I took the envelope and knocked lightly on his door. I stuck my head in. "Just me."

Julian smiled and turned his attention from his computer screen to me. "What can I do for you?"

I took the seat I'd sat in before. "Well, we came across this letter and there's no postage. So I was wondering if maybe I could pay for a stamp? Or keep it aside and I'll bring a stamp with me tomorrow?"

"Oh."

"Well, it's a birthday card to a little girl and the lady who wrote it is her nan, and the message is sweet and you can tell from the writing that she's like two hundred years old, and I'd hate to think that her card and the ten dollars doesn't make it. She's probably on a pension or something and ten dollars is a lot of money when you don't have any. I asked Cherry, but she said we didn't really do this kind of thing, like pay for it ourselves, but the fact we can send a bill to an eight-year-old girl to pay for her grandma's mail is a pretty harsh life lesson to learn at eight. Like hey, Elsa, you wanna buy this *Frozen* pencil case with your birthday money? Oh wait, you can't because the horrible postal people made you pay for a stamp when it was not your fault, so instead of ten dollars you only have nine . . . oh wait, plus the admin fee. You know, I should probably call my father and ask him what the fuck because—"

Julian raised an eyebrow.

Ooops.

"Oh shit, did I swear? Sorry, I didn't mean to. I do apologise for that. Sorry. I think I just did it again when I said shit. I said it again. You make me nervous. Sorry."

He fought a smile. "We don't make a habit of paying for any mail that comes through without adequate postage."

"But it's not against policy? So if I wanted to do it, I could?"

"You could."

I grinned. "Yay!"

God help me, I just said yay.

"I mean, that's awesome." I gave a nod, regaining my composure. "I'll bring in a stamp tomorrow." Then I looked at the envelope. "Can I, uh, can I leave this here with you so it doesn't get lost or thrown into the pile that's gonna send a repo man to an eight-year-old girl on her birthday?"

Julian did smile this time. "Okay, so we don't send a repo man. Yes, you can leave it in here. I'm sure Elsa will appreciate your efforts, because who doesn't want a *Frozen* pencil case."

I grinned at him. "Exactly."

"And as for the swearing," he added.

"Oh, I really am sorry about that."

"Why do I make you nervous?"

I could feel my face burning. "Oh, no reason. I don't know. Because you're my boss and I don't want you to fire me. I like my job here, and to be honest, I'm always nervous around people I find attractive—"

Oh hell, I did not just say that. Stop talking, Malachi, stop talking, stop fucking talking.

"—so it's not even really my fault. Elsa and I are the victims here." I held up the envelope like a shield and I stood up. "Elsa is a victim of the system though. I'm more of a victim of my own idiocy. If you read my CV, you'd have seen self-sabotage was on my list of personal skills. I don't need to even try; it just comes naturally. I'm really trying to shut up but . . ."

I didn't even realise I was backing out toward the door.

"Malachi?"

"Yes?"

"The envelope?"

I was still holding it. "Yes?"

"Did you want to leave it in here?"

"Yes, yes, I did. I'll just put it over here out of the way, on the shelf next to the letters you couldn't bring yourself to destroy." I read the top envelope. The writing was faded, the paper old. "The Dearest Milton James letters."

I backed out again toward the door. "Okay, well, this has been mortifying," I mumbled and backed out, still facing him, and banged into the door frame before I could escape and pull the door shut.

I think I heard Julian chuckle.

That went so well.

Totally nailed it, Malachi.

Fuck.

CHAPTER FOUR

MY NEW MISSION, I decided, was to avoid Julian at all costs. Because the ground wouldn't be so polite as to open up and swallow me whole, my only option was to pretend I didn't just tell him I thought he was attractive and to avoid him.

I slunk back to Cherry's desk. She was on the phone to a customer who never received a parcel. Luckily she had a tracking number so I offered to run down to aisle E-F and find it for her. And then I offered to find something else, and then another parcel, and another, anything to not be near Julian's office should he come out. And running off to find random parcels for a few hours gave me a good excuse to become familiar with the aisles and what went where.

But mostly to avoid Julian.

Because telling your boss on the second day of your employment that you found him attractive was not a good thing. It was a horrifying thing.

I wasn't lying though. The man was damn fine, despite all the beige. Behind those glasses were pretty eyes, and his lips were a faint pink colour that looked the right amount of soft.

This was going to end in disaster.

I had to get those stupid quiet-but-kinky professor vibes out of my head.

Soon it was lunch though, and I managed to sit and eat my lunch without speaking while Julian came into the breakroom and my ploy to avoid him went out the window, along with my dignity. I could feel his eyes on me a few times, though I pretended not to notice, concentrating on my phone, pretending to read something. I was still involved in conversation, kind of, but there was no way I could make eye contact with him.

Until he sat down beside me. "How are you finding it?" His deep voice rumbled right through me.

"Oh," I said, almost jumping out of my seat. I turned my phone over so it was screen-down on the table. "Yeah, it's fine. I'm still liking it, which is a surprise. I wasn't sure what to expect, but it's kinda cool."

"I'm glad."

I wiped my hands on my thighs. "Yeah, though I think my dad was more surprised than me. That I liked my first day, that is. He thought I was joking, naturally. But I said, no, I actually think I like it. He was a bit stunned but I told him we'd see how I get through day two before he got too excited."

Julian smiled as he sipped his coffee. "And how's day two working out for you so far?"

"Pretty good. Cherry's cool, and I'm trying not to talk too much. Though there was the verbiage diarrhoea in your office earlier. That didn't go too well. Sorry about that."

He chuckled and sipped his drink. "Don't apologise. I'm

glad you're liking it here. You seem to fit in well. I hope you decide to stay."

Oh.

Okay then.

"We'll see how day two pans out," I offered lamely, sure my face was on fire.

And day two panned out okay.

Same with day three. True to my word, I brought in a stamp for Elsa's birthday card and put it back out for circulation. It made me feel good; honestly the best dollar I'd ever spent.

Day four flew by, productive and fun. I spent the day with Theo, and he was nice. His sense of humour was a bit cringe, but he was actually a really nice guy.

Day five passed in a blur. I spent the morning with Denise, and she was totally cool, but I spent the afternoon at my own desk doing my own records and returns. It was kinda fun.

I was looking forward to the weekend though. Just to chill, maybe hit a bar or go out for dinner or something. I'd have to go grocery shopping again, do some laundry like a grown-up, and maybe even go and see my mum.

I was thinking of all the things I needed to do as I was finishing up on Friday evening, until I got to the door and realised it was raining. Bloody hell. Well, nothing like running to the bus stop in the rain . . .

"Malachi," a deep voice said.

I jumped. Julian was right behind me. "Oh. Hey."

"Need a lift somewhere?"

"Nah . . ." I checked my phone. I had five minutes before the bus came. "I'll just wait for the rain to ease up a bit before I run for the bus."

"It's really no problem," he murmured. "Which direction are you?"

"Newtown."

"It's on the way. Come on."

Some of the night shift crew were arriving, running in with their coats above their heads. Julian said hello to them, then stood aside and opened his umbrella. "My car's this way."

Shit.

"Oh, okay."

His car was parked around the side of the building, and funnily enough, it wasn't beige. It was a blue mid-sized SUV type thing—I wasn't good with car brands. I hadn't expected him to have that kind of car though. I thought he'd have a sensible brown sedan, but no. He walked me to the passenger door and opened it for me as the rain got heavier. I slid into the seat and he quickly shut the door and ran around to the driver's side. Once he was in and had his umbrella folded away, he smiled. "I do love the rain," he said.

Wow, small talk. Okay. "Same. Except when I need to get to the bus stop. Thank you for doing this. You certainly didn't have to."

"It's no problem."

He started the car and backed out of his spot. "So, whereabouts in Newtown?"

"Campbell Street. But anywhere on the main drag is fine. It's all narrow one-way streets, and traffic is shit at this time of day."

"It's fine," he replied, super casual. Nothing seemed to faze him at all.

"You really have your shit together, don't you?" I asked, not really meaning to say that out loud. "I mean, you can't be that much older than me, and yet you have your own car, you're the boss at work. How does one become the boss of the Dead Letter Office?"

"The Mail Recovery Centre?"

"Yeah, sorry." I still thought the Dead Letter Office sounded cooler, but okay.

"I began in the admin centre of head office as an intern straight out of high school."

Oh god. "So you know my father?"

He nodded. "Not well, obviously. Though certainly by name and reputation. I've met him several times."

I sighed. "I never found anywhere I really fit in," I admitted. "I get bored easily, and I'd rather chop and change and be happy than stick to one job I hated just for the stability."

"You fit in with us okay?" He looked at me and then back to the traffic ahead. The windscreen wipers were working overtime, red brake lights in front of us were smeared, and the grey skies were low.

"I think I do. And I do like the work. It's interesting and rewarding."

"Like sending off a birthday card with ten dollars in it from a grandma who forgot the stamp?"

"Exactly." I shrugged. "Though everyone probably thought I was crazy."

"No. I didn't think that. I thought it was sweet." He shifted in his seat. "I think it shows that you're in the right job. Maybe you found the place where you fit in."

I studied his side profile for a second. It was just as sexy as his whole face, front-on. "I hope so. I'm even starting to think that maybe Paul isn't a trucker slash serial killer."

Julian laughed; his eyes were warm and he had the

cutest laugh lines. And it made my heart feel two sizes too big for my ribs.

"Paul?" He said, smiling. "Highly doubt he's a serial killer, though I can see maybe why you'd think that."

"Ah, highly doubt is not ruling out the possibility."

Julian chuckled. "Paul's a nice guy. A bit out there, but we're all a little left of mainstream."

"Is that why you think I fit in?" I was trying to decide if I should be offended, but he was spot on. I'd never been mainstream. I'd never wanted to be.

Julian nodded without any sense of remorse or apology. "Yes."

He was so confident, so absolutely sure of himself. Not in a conceited way, but in a sexy way, and the only thing I was absolutely sure of was that it was going to land me in trouble.

"Can I ask you something?" I asked.

He kept his eyes on the road but I noticed there was a slight flinch in his eyes. "Sure."

"What's the story behind those letters? In your office. The Milton James letters. You said there was a story behind them and they've sat in your office for years, so clearly they mean something."

"They, uh . . ." And for the first time, he seemed unsure. "They do mean something."

"I'm sorry. You don't have to tell me. I didn't realise it was personal or private. I shouldn't have asked. I'm always opening my mouth and just shoving my whole foot in."

Julian shot me a half-smile. "It's okay. I was going to say it wasn't personal or private, but they are. Those letters were kept in a pile long before I began working there. They'd been set aside in the early 1970s, I believe, then lost. Found again in the 2010s in the back of the old storage facility when they moved everything from the old ware-house to the new facility where we are today. And Cheryl, the manager before me, thought they were interesting, so she kept them."

"What's in them?"

But Julian couldn't answer. He had to slow down for pedestrians and pulled into my street. "Which one's yours?"

"The white building, next block." It was pelting down now. "I really appreciate this."

"You're welcome." He pulled up the best he could, given all the cars parked on the left side, and I was out of time. "You didn't tell me what was in the letters."

A car beeped behind us and Julian's eyes went from the rear-vision mirror to me. "Next time."

"Yeah, shit, sorry. Thanks again. And . . ." I grabbed the door handle. "Have a great weekend doing whatever it is you do."

He smiled. "See you Monday."

"Yes, you will."

I threw open the door and climbed out into the rain. By the time I got to the stoop of the entrance to my block of flats and turned around, he was gone.

MONDAY. Why did everyone hate Mondays? I'd never been so excited for a Monday in all my life. I even arrived early. Well, the bus got in fifteen minutes early and it was either be early or be late, so I opted for early.

Everyone arrived around the same time, and we sat in the breakroom drinking awful coffee and talking about our weekends.

Paul had cooked some stews and gone hiking in the

national park. And with that confession, paired with the army-green coat he was sporting, the serial-killer vibe was back.

Denise had gone to a family gatho at the in-laws. Her girlfriend's mum's seventieth birthday apparently, and they were too hungover yesterday to do much of anything.

Theo went to his nephew's soccer game on Saturday morning, took his dad to Bunnings on Saturday arvo, watched the double Stallone feature on Channel 10 on Saturday night, helped his mum at the grocery store on Sunday, and . . .

Oh my word, he gave every conversation he had, every detail of every goddamn minute. I'd finished my first coffee and was onto my second by the time Theo wrapped up all the inadvertent reasons why he was single and still living with his parents.

"What about you, Cherry?" I asked.

Everyone looked stricken for a second, as though it was an unspoken rule that no one asked Cherry how her weekend went.

Cherry studied me for a second, her gothic expression stoic. "Not much," she replied. "There was a light exhibition at the Paddington gallery. The artist expresses the space of negative light. It was cool."

"Oh my god," I said. "Is that the Blue Door Gallery in Paddington? I love that place. My friend took me to see the charcoal exhibition last year. I hadn't wanted to go, but Moni explained it was charcoal drawings of the nude male form. She really should have led with that. Anyway, I now have a better appreciation of art."

Cherry gave a small smile. "I saw that one."

"What about you, Malachi?" Paul asked. "What did you get up to? Can see you changed your hair."

"Oh, yeah," I said, subconsciously touching the chunk of hair that was now purple amidst the black. "Needed a colour to go over the blue. Plus it gave me an excuse to wear this."

My shirt was dark purple, my shoes were lilac. I lifted my foot so they could all see.

"Any hot dates?" Denise asked with a wink at the same time that Julian walked in. He went straight to the kitchenette and proceeded to make himself a coffee. I proceeded to pretend not to check him out.

I sipped my coffee. "No. Unfortunately my standards exceed the availability pool. It's been that way for a while now."

"Oh, no app hook-ups like everyone else these days?" Denise said, glancing pointedly at Julian's back.

What the hell kinda game was she playing?

I shook my head. "Oh no, not for me. I tried the online thing once. It was very misleading. I mean, it wasn't a dating app exactly, but H&M sent a notification to my phone that said *two tops for the price of one*, and believe me, that was not the case."

Julian choked on his first sip of coffee. Denise roared laughing. Paul snorted; Cherry smiled. Theo didn't get it.

I beamed at them. "The lady at H&M was very confused when I explained and requested a raincheck on the real thing and asked me not to call her again. So I'll be sticking to finding suitable guys at the normal places. Like coffee shops and libraries. Which is where they hang out, apparently. Not that I would know. I met all my exes in nightclubs or bathroom stalls."

"Classy," Denise replied.

"Did you get it?" Theo asked.

Lord, that was a loaded question. I baulked. "Get what?"

"The raincheck," he replied, so innocent. And naïve. And possibly dim. "They have to honour them, you know. You should check their store policy. If they advertised two tops for the price of one . . ."

I took my cup to the sink and leaned against the counter, half facing Julian who had his cup to his mouth to hide his smirk.

"Oh no, Theo. It was fine," I replied. "Believe me, one top is more than enough."

Julian pushed off, taking long strides to the door. "Work time," he said before he disappeared with his coffee into his office.

Denise laughed again, we washed our cups, and we all began our workday. I was on my own now. At my own desk with my own cage trolley of returns and a huge list of inventory to get through. There was a lot to get done, and even though I did miss helping one of the others, I kinda liked being able to do it on my own too.

It was still fun and rewarding.

I got plenty logged and filed, but I found the correct owners for a good portion of them too. And that felt good. Most were incorrect addresses, but a quick google and a phone call later, the parcels were re-addressed and put back into the system.

I got to open a bunch of parcels, which was fun. It was like opening presents all day long except they don't belong to you and you don't get to keep them, but it was the opening part that was fun. It was exciting! Most of the time it was just clothing or shoes, homewares, and a surprising amount of electronics. But sometimes it was personal stuff like photos or jewellery.

"Oh, I got another one," Cherry said, louder than I'd ever heard her speak.

"Another what?" I asked, standing up to get a better view.

Denise and Paul walked over and peered into the box she was holding.

Cherry lifted out an arm.

A lifelike human arm with a hand.

"It's an old prosthetic arm, like from the 1950s or some-thing," Paul said. "Cool."

Okay, we were definitely back at the creepy serial-killer vibes.

"It's a left," Denise noted. "What was the other one you got?"

"A right forearm and a left leg below the knee," Cherry replied.

"Wait," I said, horrified. "This is not your first?"

Cherry shook her head. "Nope."

"Is someone mailing a body in pieces?" I asked, my voice slightly higher than normal. "Because that's horrifying."

"On the bright side," Paul mused, "at least it's not the head."

Then, of course, Denise had to give us all her imperson-ation from the movie *Seven* with Brad Pitt's 'what's in the box' scene. She actually did a pretty good job . . .

But then Paul had to take the arm and rub it with his finger. "It puts the lotion on the skin," he said, and I shud-dered from the top of my head right down to my lilac fucking boots.

"Nope, nope, nope, nope," I mumbled, walking back-wards, and I bumped right into Julian.

Of course, I screamed.

It was shrill enough to scare the pigeons off the roof, apparently. Or maybe that was Denise's loud laughter. I couldn't be sure.

But Julian grabbed my elbow in a way that wasn't exactly terrible. "Are you okay?" he asked. That deep voice dripped like fucking honey.

"Oh, yeah," I said with my hand to my forehead. "Just had nightmares for a year about Buffalo Bill after I watched *Silence of the Lambs*. Well, actually, the nightmares were more about that human skin suit he was sewing, and to be honest, I'm not sure how I feel about working with a serial killer?"

We both looked over at Paul and he was now raking the prosthetic hand through his hair. "Paul, please give the limb back to Cherry," Julian said, like it wasn't totally weird.

Paul grinned like Jame Gumb. "You mean, give her a hand."

Denise laughed. Cherry rolled her eyes.

"Sorry, Malachi, didn't mean to scare you. It was just a little 'armless joke," Paul added. But he did give Cherry back the prosthetic arm and went back to his desk. He collected a parcel and whistled as he disappeared down the aisles.

I realised two things at once. One, Julian still had his hand on my arm, and two, something Cherry said.

"Uh, Cherry, did you say you have another one? As in this is not the first arm you've found in the mail?"

Cherry wasn't even fazed. Not one bit. "Nope. I've had a foot, a left arm from the shoulder, and a right arm from the elbow."

Speaking of elbows . . . the mention of the word must have made Julian realise he was still holding my arm and he let go.

"What the hell is wrong with people?" I asked. "Why are they shipping fake body parts?"

Cherry found a piece of paper in the box. "Here's an order form with a purchase slip. eBay," she said like that explained everything. "Sometimes it's mannequin parts."

I grimaced. "I do *not* want to know."

Julian was watching me, somewhat amused. "Body parts freak you out?"

"It's more fake body parts, like puppets." I shuddered.

"Puppets?"

I made a gagging sound. "Honestly think I'd prefer a real arm in the box. Except then Paul would probably take it home for the skin suit he's making."

Julian pressed his lips together so he didn't smile. "Uh, I'm almost one hundred per cent certain he's *not* a serial killer."

I nodded slowly. "Almost certain. So you're basically saying the chances are unlikely but unequivocally can never be zero. Got it."

"That's not what I said."

"That's what I heard."

He tilted his head ever so slightly, as if he was trying to figure something out but then like he remembered where he was, and a switch was flipped. He shook his head a little and straightened up. "So, uh, how's your quota coming along today??"

Oh, work. Right. "Yeah, pretty good." I went to my desk and held up my clipboard to show him. "Mostly done."

"Good," he said, his eyes warm behind his glasses. "If you have any questions, just ask me."

He disappeared into his office and I got back to work, disappointed that I didn't have anything I could knock on his office door and ask him. Anything just to speak to him again, to hear that low baritone voice. I could still feel where he'd touched my arm.

I was kinda bummed that I didn't get to see him again for the rest of the day. But soon it was knock-off time, so we all grabbed our things, said our round of goodbyes, and as I was walking out, that deep honey voice caught me.

"Need a lift home?"

I turned to find Julian smiling, carrying a messenger bag. Christ, how did that make him cuter?

"You don't have to do that," I said. "The bus is fine. And by fine, I mean it's crowded and it smells funky. But at least it's not raining. The rain takes the smell to a whole new level of gross."

He laughed. "Come on. Your place is on the way," he said, walking toward his car, just expecting me to follow.

I wanted to tell him no. I was just about to open my mouth and tell him thanks but no thanks—as much as I wanted to go with him . . . and I really did want to—but then he stopped and turned, a confused frown on his face.

"It's fine if you'd rather not," he said.

"No, I just don't want to be an inconvenience," I said. "I have this aversion to inconveniencing people, where I'd prefer to do literally anything other than that."

He checked his watch. "Well, you'd best hurry if you want to catch the . . ."

The bus that just drove past the gate.

He watched it go. "Oh."

I sighed. "Well, shit. Uh, if the offer still stands for the lift . . ."

He laughed. "Get in."

CHAPTER FIVE

"I DO APPRECIATE THIS," I said, trying not to feel awkward.

He gave me a sweet smile as he backed the car out of the parking spot. "I don't mind one bit."

"So, about Paul," I began. "With the whole serial-killer vibe he has going on. I don't think he's actually a serial killer. I think he's weird. But not creepy. I mean, he is a bit creepy. But not *creepy* creepy. And if he were a real serial killer, I think I'd get the *creepy*-creepy vibes, ya know?"

Julian chuckled. "I'm glad you no longer think of him like that. He's a little weird, granted. I can imagine him watching *X-Files* marathons or secretly having government conspiracy theories, perhaps? But not a serial killer." He drove so smoothly, so confidently, and I found that very attractive. "He's actually a nice guy."

Nice guy? "Uh. The *Silence of the Lambs* impression was a little too real for him to fall under the nice category. I've lessened the likelihood of him being a serial killer, but I think nice might be subjective. Helpful, maybe. Polite or agreeable, yes. But nice?"

He shot me a smile. "He was just messing with you. I think he likes you."

My voice came out two octaves higher. "Likes me?"

"Not like that."

"Good. I mean, yes, good." I patted my hair down. "I am a total catch though." Then I remembered my conversation in the breakroom this morning. "Oh, about what I said this morning when we were having coffee and I said that thing . . . about the tops being two for one, I'm sorry if that was out of line. I tend to say stuff that I realise I shouldn't have said, generally right after I've said them."

He looked at me with a slow-spreading smile. "It probably wasn't work-appropriate." Then he shrugged. "But it was funny."

"Just so you know, I didn't actually call the store to ask about a raincheck. As well as saying inappropriately timed things, I tend to try and make people laugh when I'm nervous." I made a face. "I'm sure there's a whole section of psychological journals written on using humour for deflection of vulnerability, or whatever. It's just easier than being awkward, and knowing you're awkward, and knowing you make other people awkward."

He frowned. "Are you nervous now? You're doing that nervous rambling thing. I don't mean to make you uncomfortable by offering you a lift home."

Oh shit.

"No, no. God. That's not why I'm nervous. I mean, I'm not nervous." Why couldn't I just shut my mouth? "Well, I am a bit. But you make me nervous. Being around attractive people makes me nervous. It always has. Which probably explains my disastrous attempt at dating anyone I actually like. I just can't stop myself from putting my foot in it. Like now."

Christ, Malachi, stop talking.

Stop. Talking.

Stop.

Julian barked out a disbelieving laugh. "Attractive people? I'm not attractive people."

I stared at him. *Did I call him attractive? Again? Fuck. I think I did.*

Dear brain,

Please disengage all talking operations. Actually, just shut down all mouth functionality. Cease all operations. Error 404, file not found, something to make it stop. I'd even take a fatal error, blue screen of death right now . . .

"You okay?" he asked. "You look kinda green."

I put my hand to my forehead. "I'm trying not to talk. Because when I open my mouth, stupid shit comes out. As I'm sure you just witnessed. Exhibit A in all its glory."

He surprised me by laughing. And not laughing at me. His eyes were warm, as though he found me endearing.

Great.

"I'm sorry," I said, wiping my hands down my thighs, trying not to be as awkward as I felt. I realised then that we hadn't moved in a while. "Wow, traffic's bad today."

"I think there's roadwork ahead," he offered.

Fucking awesome. The trip home was not only painfully uncomfortable but also the longest of my life.

I wracked my brain trying to think of something to change the subject with . . .

"Oh, those letters in your office," I said. "The ones addressed to Milton James."

"Dearest Milton James."

"Yeah, those. You said you tried to find the owners?"

He pursed his lips and his hand on the steering wheel tightened. "I did."

"But you had no luck?"

He shook his head and offered a sad smile. "No."

"Maybe we could try?" I said. "I mean, all of us. At the office. Cherry's good at obscure things, and I've had some luck. Even though I've only been there a week. But maybe we could have another go and see what we can come up with."

He made a face, almost pained. "I don't know if that's a good idea."

"Why not? You've read the letters, right? To try and find information."

He gave a small nod. "The letters are . . . the letters are very personal. And given their sensitive nature and the time in which they were written, I just think maybe we're best to leave them be."

I frowned at that. "Oh. Are they sad?"

Julian inhaled slowly and shook his head. "No, they're actually lovely. Beautiful, even."

"They're love letters?"

He smiled, brown eyes shining, and he nodded. "Love letters. From one man to another."

I put my hand to my heart. "They're gay love letters?"

Julian met my gaze and his smile was as sweet as it was sad. "Yes."

"Oh my god," I said, my excitement getting the better of me. "That's awesome!"

Julian stared out at the stopped traffic for a while, and we finally began to drive forward. But he didn't say anything and I thought back to what he'd said earlier.

'Given their sensitive nature and the time in which they were written, I just think maybe we're best to leave them be.'

Oh.

"The time in which they were written," I repeated. "It was the early seventies, right? It was a forbidden love."

Julian nodded. "Very much so."

My heart sank. "That's so sad."

"It is sad." He sighed but ended it with a smile. "They're very beautifully written though."

I understood then. "And you think maybe they're not supposed to ever find their way home."

Julian met my gaze and his stare burned into me, intense and honest. He shook his head, as if breaking some trance, then let out a breath and focused on the traffic for a while. "A lot of time has passed. I wonder if they surfaced now if they'd do more harm than good." He swallowed, his voice rough. "Imagine finding an elderly man who then has to explain to his wife of fifty years why he wrote that kind of letter to a man."

"You're worried it might out him?"

Julian nodded. "I'd never be able to forgive myself."

I shrank back in my seat, feeling a sadness and regret for all those gay folks who paved the way for my generation. For how hard life must have been for them. It wasn't easy for us now, and for some it would never be. But at least we were no longer illegal. It made my heart hurt.

It also gave me a new appreciation for Julian.

"You're very kind," I offered. "For thinking of them over your duty to see the mail delivered."

"I did look for them. I did search," he added. "It's not like I didn't try. But there really wasn't much to go by, and I wasn't too sad when I came up empty."

I sighed. "I can appreciate that."

Traffic was moving a bit faster now, and from as awkward as it was before, I didn't want this car ride to be over. "What was the name of the guy who wrote the letters? Did he sign them?"

Julian shook his head. "In one letter he signs off with a name, but I don't know if it's a real name or completely fictional."

"But you know it was a man?"

"Oh, yes. He writes of stolen kisses in the dark, of feeling stubble against his own, of his rough hands. Of having to go through the pretence of dating a girl when all he wants is to be with him."

I put my hand to my cheek and swooned a little. "Oh, my heart! How romantic!"

Julian finally smiled. "Very."

He turned onto my street and I wished we had more time. "I really do appreciate the lift," I said as he slowed down at my apartment building.

"I don't mind at all. I enjoy the company." His cheeks tinted pink as if admitting that was embarrassing.

"I enjoy your company too," I said, probably misreading the situation completely. He said *the* company, I said *his* company. But it wasn't a lie. "And thank you for telling me about the letters. I hope Milton and his secret man found some happiness. But like you said, sometimes it is best to let sleeping dogs lie." I unbuckled my seatbelt and put my hand on the door handle. "And sometimes our truths are best kept quiet. Especially when it's not our secret to tell."

He didn't say anything to that, so I took it as my cue to leave. "Have a good night, Julian. See you tomorrow." Then because my brain was my brain, it offloaded another round of embarrassment. "And tomorrow, we can just pretend that I never said you were attractive again. Totally never happened. Even if it is true, we're just gonna pretend I never said it out loud."

He smiled as I got out of his car. "See you tomorrow."

HE KEPT up his end of the bargain. The next day, he did pretend that I'd never said he was attractive. And the day after that. He never mentioned it at all. He smiled at me, was polite, but there was no conversation and no offers for a lift home. He was ever the professional.

I kept my head down at work. I got through my long lists of work to do, and I still enjoyed it. In fact, I think I enjoyed it a little more every day.

Paul was still weird. He made no more *Silence of the Lambs* jokes, thankfully. Theo was still nice as hell, and every time I heard Denise's rough bark of laughter from somewhere in the warehouse, I would smile.

But Cherry was my favourite. Her introverted goth matched my extroverted rainbow like two sides of one coin. I found myself drawn to her more than the others, and I could be so bold as to say we were becoming friends. We would walk to the bus stop together after work, even sit together if the seating allowed.

I got the feeling she didn't friend anyone too easily. Much like I didn't. But when we did find someone that appreciated our quirkiness, it was a real thing.

But Julian . . .

I found myself looking for him and being hyperaware when he came out of his office. And when he joined us in the breakroom for lunch. I sat with Cherry, and every time Julian looked my way, it felt like a laser of intense heat.

Like it tore up everything in its path to find me.

But he never offered me another lift home.

Which was fine. I could catch the bus like a normal person. Like I'd done all my life. It was no big deal.

I couldn't deny it made me sad. Did my awkwardness repel him? Probably. Did me telling him I found him attractive cross a professional line? Most likely. Did it make him uneasy around me? Obviously, yes. And it shouldn't have surprised me because this was usually how things went for me.

I should have been used to it, but it still stung.

On Thursday, three days after he drove me home, I got to work ten minutes early like I always did. Just like everyone did. As I was making my first coffee, Paul came in with a cake.

"Is it someone's birthday?" I asked brightly. Cake was always a reason to be excited.

He put the cake on the table underneath the shrine to Glenda. It was a cat-shaped cake, I realised. "It's Glenda's birthday," Paul replied.

Oh.

Denise helped with the candles, Cherry got some plates and a knife from the cupboard, and Julian walked in just as Theo counted us all in to sing the 'Happy Birthday' song like he was conducting an orchestra.

The whole thing was weird.

But everyone here was some kind of weird so I went with it like it was completely normal.

"Happy birthday, Glenda!" they all toasted in various manners, lifting their coffees and cake to the shrine on the wall.

"Glenda always brought in a cat cake," Theo told me as he handed me a plate with a slice of the cat's arse on it.

"Thanks," I said with a befuddled smile. The cat's arse? What was that supposed to mean?

"I was gonna make it red velvet," Paul said way too cheerfully. "So it looked like it bled when we cut into it."

Oh god.

"But," he continued, "I figured after the 'it rubs the lotion' comment, I probably shouldn't."

I sighed. He really was taking the piss. "Just so you know, that movie freaked me out so much. Almost as much as *Grease 2*."

Paul tilted his head. "*Grease 2*?"

"Yes, the movie." I shuddered as I stuck my fork into the cat's arse and shovelled it into my mouth before I could tell them that I almost considered heterosexuality because of Michelle Pfeiffer singing on the back of a motorbike. "Let me just say. It was not the experience I was expecting. John Travolta as Danny Zuko in the first *Grease*, on the other hand . . ."

Julian shot me a look, so I shovelled more cake into my stupid face hole while he made himself a coffee. He took the plate of cake Theo offered him and made his way back to the door. He stopped and looked at me. "Malachi, do you have a moment?"

Well, this is going to be good.

"Sure," I said brightly despite the sense of dread in my belly. "One sec. I'll just . . ." *shove in the last of my cake.*

If he was impressed by my ability to unhinge my jaw, open wide, and take in an obscene amount of food, he hid it well.

I could also open my throat and swallow at the same time, but I figured now was not the time to bring that up . . .

I quickly scrubbed my coffee cup, wondering if it'd be the last time I'd ever use it. I was beginning to like the puce colour and I didn't want to get fired from this job.

I loved this job.

And I'd never loved any job.

"Do you think he's gonna fire me?" I asked Cherry, who was making herself a second coffee.

She blinked, stunned. "What for?"

"For being me. I say stupid shit. I need to stop saying stupid shit."

She put her hand on my arm. "Don't think like that. You being you is what makes you fit in here. But if you keep him waiting . . ."

"Oh, right." I made a face. "Good point."

With a sinking stomach and a sigh, I knocked on his door. "Hey. You wanted to see me?"

Julian nodded, finishing his mouthful of cake. He pushed his plate away, licked his lips, and smiled. "Come in."

I was gonna need a minute to save that mental imagery masterpiece.

"Is everything okay?" I asked, sitting across from him. Then I leaned in and whispered. "Does this have anything to do with me thinking *Grease* 2 is an abomination? Because if you're a fan . . ."

"What? No."

"Thank god. Wait. Does this have anything to do with me calling you attractive twice now? Because I would apologise. Reluctantly, because I'm a firm believer in preaching the truth. But if it would make you feel better . . . and if it would help me keep this job because I actually really like working here. It's the first job I've ever had that I think I love and I'd really appreciate not being fired, if that's okay."

He blinked. "Ah, no." Then he laughed. "I'm glad you're enjoying your work."

"Yes, I am! Well, I ate the arse of a cat cake this morning and we toasted the birth of a dead woman whom I never met, and that wasn't even the weirdest part of my morning."

Julian met my eyes and laughed. "Do I want to know what the weirdest part of your morning was?" He glanced at the clock on the wall. "Considering it's not even 9am."

"I catch public transport." I shrugged. "Weird is a given. Though this morning's specialty was what I could only assume was the walk of shame for a guy wearing a silver sequin dress and dirty work boots. He had amazing calf and thigh muscles, and from his shoulders and hands, I think maybe he's in construction. I was going to ask where he kept his wallet, but he smelled of bourbon and regret and I didn't want to wear his vomit."

Julian's smile widened. "I see."

"I'm trying not to say stupid shit," I blurted out. "But again, with the handsome-nervous thing. God, I just said shit. Am I fired?"

"Fired? No, not at all." He pursed his lips to hide his smile, though his eyes gave away a bit too much.

Holy shit.

He was looking at me like that. Like he was into me . . . If we were in a bar, I'd bet a few vodka martinis sure I was getting some.

But we weren't in a bar.

We were at work.

But those honey-brown eyes were shining at me some kind of way.

My belly swooped and fluttered with butterflies, and I let out a slow breath. "You wanted to see me about something? And if I'm not getting fired . . ."

"Oh, yes, right." He cleared his throat and sat forward

in his seat. "What you said the other day in the car. It struck a chord with me."

I tried to think back.

"I said a lot, and I'm going to need you to narrow that down for me. I have a verbiage condition around attractive people. As we've discussed a few times now."

His smile produced a dimple.

A fucking dimple.

Okay then.

Hang up my lilac boots and cover me in carnations. It's all over for me.

Then, because I wasn't dead enough, the fucker took off his glasses. He just took them off and slid them onto his desk like he took out a machete and cut me in half.

That's how dead I was.

He mowed me down in my fucking seat.

"You said sometimes our truths are best kept quiet." He bit his bottom lip and I died for the third time in two minutes. "Actually, you said sometimes our truths are best kept quiet, especially when it's not our secret to tell."

I blinked, surprised, to be honest, that my eyeballs still worked.

"I'm sorry, what?" My voice squeaked. Clearly my brain and my mouth were struggling.

Who knew? Who knew that I could fly past the word-vomit stage into the speechless idiot stage with a dimple and the removal of glasses?

Who fucking knew?

Julian rubbed his thumb and forefinger into his eye sockets and sighed. "I haven't been able to stop thinking about that."

"Okay." I really wasn't following. "And?"

He sighed. "The letters. The Dearest Milton James letters."

"Oh." I looked over to where the letters had sat to find them not there. Before I could ask where they were, he produced them like magic and sat them right in the middle of his desk.

"I think we should try and find Milton James."

CHAPTER SIX

———————

I CLAPPED my hands together and gasped. "For real?"

He nodded.

"And I thought eating the butthole of a cat cake was going to be the highlight of my day."

Julian snorted.

"Sorry."

"I thought the guy wearing a sequin dress on the bus was the highlight of your day."

"That was the weirdest. Though honestly, given I still have a return trip to make yet today, that door is still open. The afternoon bus adventures to home are usually the best for weird. I'll let you know tomorrow how it went."

Julian smiled warmly. He met my eyes and didn't look away for a few beats too long.

It did twirly things to my stomach.

"So how do we do this?" I asked before I let my nerves get the better of me. "Because my job list is usually chockers, as I'm sure you know. But I can try to fit it in."

Julian shifted in his seat, looking slightly uncomfortable.

"I know you're busy. I am too. I have reports and budgets to get through. But I thought between the two of us . . ."

The two of us. Working together. Me and Mr Sexy.

He chewed on the inside of his lip, his brows furrowed. "How are you at keeping secrets?"

I sat forward, eyes wide, excited. "Absolutely terrible. Do not tell me anything."

Julian laughed. "I kinda figured that'd be the case."

Oh. "Is that . . . um, what?"

He smirked at me. "Malachi, in the short time I've known you, you've told me twice that you are honest to a fault, and you've displayed, on several occasions, the ability of spectacular word verbiage."

"Oh." I relaxed. "That's all true."

Julian put his hand on the stack of Dear Milton James letters. "Now, about these. I'm fine with the others knowing." He gave a pointed glance to the door. "So you don't have to lie about it. Though I'd rather no one else get involved. These letters are quite personal and—" He sighed. "It would feel like a violation, of sorts. If we can even find Mr James or the man who sent the letters, which is unlikely. I know that sounds a little weird, but . . ."

"But the nature of the letters calls for discretion," I offered.

Julian nodded slowly. "Yes. If we do find the sender or recipient, I'd like to be able to reassure them that no one else read the letters."

I found myself smiling at him. "That's very decent of you."

He smiled right back and did that staring thing that pinned me to my seat. Christ, was it hot in here all of a sudden?

"The thing is," Julian added, his voice low, "I don't

know if these letters should leave this office. Or the premises, at least. Should they be lost or damaged outside of this building. They can't be replaced."

It was my turn to nod. "Okay. So how do we . . . ?"

"You can read them in here." His tone was his boss voice, deeper and final. My inner twink-who-wants-a-daddy sat up and took notice.

"Okay. Sure."

I would have agreed to him suggesting anything when he used that voice.

"Or at your desk, if you'd prefer." His voice was softer, relenting.

"Oh no, in here's fine."

His lips twitched. "Did you want to start today?"

"Yes." I might have answered a little too quickly. "Sounds great."

"You'll need to read them first, obviously."

"Then that's what I'll start on."

His phone rang, which made me glance at the clock. It was now after nine and I was supposed to be out on the floor. I stood up. "Shit. I mean, oops. I'm late." I gestured to his phone as I walked backwards to the door. "I'll let you get that and I'll just . . . I'll be back later. To read the letters. I guess. If that's what we're doing." His phone kept ringing and I stupidly kept talking. I pretended to zip my mouth and he was smiling at me by the time I forced myself out the door.

When I pulled the door closed, I leaned against it and sighed.

Cherry was at her desk and she glanced up. "Every-thing okay?"

I nodded quickly. "Yep. Super. Didn't get fired, so you know, yay, bonus."

She gave a sly smirk and rolled her eyes, as though me thinking Julian would ever fire me was ridiculous. But she never asked for any more details and I was grateful. Although Julian didn't want me to lie about what we had planned, he also didn't want it made public. Not that I could have told anyone anyway, because once I started my job list, I never even looked up until Cherry told me it was lunchtime.

The good news was that I put a pretty big dent in my work, and that would give me some time to read those letters.

And I was excited to read them. Intrigued, hella-curious, even a little nervous.

It wasn't too unusual for some of us to be milling around during our lunch break. Sometimes we sat in the break-room, but sometimes we sat at our desks and finished off some paperwork or whatever needed doing.

So I ate my lunch real quick, then knocked on Julian's door. "Hey," I said, poking my head in.

He looked from his computer screen to me and smiled, pushing his keyboard away and giving me his undivided attention. *So, that was hot.* "Come in," he replied in that deep, sexy voice of his.

"Is now a good time for me to . . . ?"

"Yes, sure. Take a seat."

"Did you have your lunch yet?" I asked, sitting across from him.

Julian smiled, his eyes an imploring brown. Christ, they could burn holes into me and I wouldn't even be mad about it. I was two seconds away from asking him to do exactly that—asking him to do something, anything, to me—when he spoke. "Not yet."

The way he looked at me, the way his deep voice rattled

right through me, it took me a second to gather my thoughts. "Is it . . . is it okay if I read through those letters now? Do you mind? Or would you rather I sit at my desk, because that's—"

"It's fine, Malachi." He stood up and it took all of my self-control to keep eye contact and not look down at his crotch. I really wanted to, but I was a very good boy and managed not to ogle what God gave him.

"I'll just go have my lunch and give you a few minutes to get reading." He picked up the pile of letters, still bound in twine, and placed them before me on his desk. "There's a few to get through, but they're in chronological order which makes it easier to follow."

I nodded, now staring at the pile of mail. Julian left me to it and I plucked at the twine, pulling the bow undone. I took the first envelope and opened it. It was old, the paper dusty and delicate. I took a second to appreciate the hand-writing. It was old-school cursive, in fancy ink, like calligraphy. No computer-generated font could replicate this. It was beautiful.

I took a deep breath and began to read.

Dearest Milton James,

I write this knowing it will never find you, and in many ways it's for the best. This way, I can write all the things I was too afraid to speak, too afraid to even admit to myself.

You'll be leaving soon. Your birthdate sealed it for you. When they called the number twenty-two, my heart broke. I've never hated a number more.

Twenty-two. Why couldn't you have been born

on the twenty-first or the twenty-third? Why was it that day?

Why was it you that got called and not me?

I'd send a thousand men in your place.

We have three weeks before you leave for Duntroon and it's not long enough.

I want to tell you what's in my heart. I want to say so much. We steal a brush of hands or a timid smile. You put your arm around my shoulder as a friend or brother might, but your touch lingers. It sears me through my shirt. Sometimes when we're alone I see the spark of want in your eyes and I dare to hope you will act upon it.

Is it wrong that I should feel this way?

Is it wrong that I daydream of you?

Is it wrong for me to want you as I should want a woman?

If it is wrong, Milton James, I'm not certain I want to be right.

I'll end this now, though I've said too much.

Signed, my love.

———————————————————————

Oh my god.

These were forbidden love letters. Between two men in a time when such things were most certainly not allowed. It was postmarked 1972.

Oh hell . . . Duntroon. Milton James was going to Duntroon in 1972 . . . He was being sent off to the Vietnam War. His birthday was the twenty-second. He was conscripted into the war.

My heart felt all kinds of heavy. I felt a little ill.

I opened the next letter.

Dearest Milton James,

Today was the best and worst day of my life. We swam in the river, as we've done a hundred times, just you and me. The sun glistened on your skin, water from your hair ran rivulets down your torso, you smiled as you laughed.

You swam to me in the water, smile wide. We wrestled like we'd done so many times before, only this time it was different.

You stopped and I stopped, our hands on each other, our bodies close.

There was fear in your eyes, hidden in the blue. I'm sure you saw the same in mine. But then, with more courage than I could ever muster, you kissed me quick.

Oh, I was so surprised, you misread my shock for horror. You tried to back away but I managed to hold you fast.

I asked you to do it again.

And you did. Warm lips in cool water, the sun burning our skin as my world stopped turning. Your hands, your mouth.

It was the best moment of my life. Everything I'd questioned about myself, about my life, was answered.

We broke apart, smiling, scared.

You didn't want to leave without doing that, you'd said. Reminding me you were leaving in two weeks. You didn't have a choice. You'd be gone and we might not ever see each other again.

And so the best moment of my life became my worst.

We walked home without another word spoken between us, even though there was so much to be said.

Signed, my love.

I quickly opened the next letter as carefully as I could.

Dearest Milton James,

I need you to know that kissing you was the best moment of my life. In my last letter I said that day was also the worst day, but now, with the gift of hindsight, I know the truth.

There'll never be another day like it.

I may never have another moment like it.

I can tell you, anonymous Milton James, that kissing another man settled something in me. Something frightening, something I'd feared for a long time. My father would dare beat it out of me if he ever knew.

No one can ever know.

I tried to hide my smile and play it cool so my cousin wouldn't suspect us when you pulled up in your dad's Marquis. You looked so handsome with your shirtsleeves rolled up and the windows down. And I imagined we were a world away as we drove out past Acacia Road to that private swimming hole. Patsy Cline on the radio, the summer coming to an end.

We had so much more privacy at the river than we ever did at the town pool.

We kissed until the sun disappeared through

the trees. Nervous and fumbling and laughing,
touching and tasting. And when you dropped me
home, I was one hundred per cent in love with you.

Signed, all my love.

Oh god. My heart was about to burst.

I hadn't even noticed Julian come back in, but he was
sitting in his seat watching me read.

"You need to tell me right now if he dies," I demanded.
"I won't be able to—"

Julian shook his head and gave me a gentle smile. "He
doesn't die."

"But he goes off to war?" I was holding the letter a little
too tight. "I don't even think I can handle that."

"Just keep reading."

"Julian, I can't deal with angst and sadness. It kills me.
I'm not kidding. I totally cry during pet insurance ads
on TV."

He chuckled.

"I mean it. I might look a little feisty on the outside, but
I am complete marshmallow on the inside."

He seemed to find that amusing. "Feisty marshmallow.
Got it."

I put the letter down. "I'm not a pretty crier, I'll have
you know. I'd like to think I could weep poetically, but no,
it's more of a snot-sobbing, ugly cry. Just so you know."

He laughed again but took pity on me. "Shame.
Weeping poetically sounds delightful. But perhaps we
should leave the rest of the letters for later."

"So he does go off to war and I'm going to blubber like
Judy Blume."

"Like who?"

"I don't know. My mum says that." I shrugged and glanced at his clock. Shoot. "God, look at the time." I neatly folded the letters and placed them in their envelopes, keeping the read letters aside and the still-unread letters in their pile. I stood up and made an apologetic face. "Yes, to leaving the letters for later, that is." I got to the door. "But just so you know, if he goes to war and dies, I'll be an emotional wreck for the foreseeable future, possibly forever. You should prepare yourself."

Julian was smiling at me as if I was the cutest thing he'd ever seen. It did very strange swoopy things to my belly, and for some strange reason, my cheeks burned hot. "Later."

I went back to work, tackling the rest of my list of lost mail to sort. There were packages of clothes, food, camping gear, a horse bridle, two very large tubes of lube and some sex toys, letters, and a lot of junk mail.

It was never boring, that was for sure.

I was making myself a pretty good success rate too, which I was proud of. My job was kinda menial in the scheme of things, but I was making a difference to some people, no matter how small, and that felt good.

I actually tested myself to see how much I could get done, how many letters and parcels I could successfully redirect, so it was so easy to lose track of time. Five o'clock came around so fast, I thought the time was wrong, and I had to run to grab my stuff so I could hurry for the bus.

I logged out of my computer, grabbed my things, and spun around only to run right into Julian.

"Oh," I said, trying not to paw him like I wanted to. I mean, I did run into him, like actually physically collided and my hands went to his chest. Which felt surprisingly hard and bulkier than I'd thought. His taupe shirt was soft, almost silk-like, and I'm telling you right now, that combination—hard muscle under silk—well, that is hotter than hell. But yes, getting back to me not pawing at him like I wanted to . . .

I took a step back and his hands went to my shoulders to steady me. "I'm sorry," he said, his voice deep and quiet. "I didn't mean to startle you."

"That's okay, my fault. I wasn't looking." I glanced around for the time but couldn't find a clock. "I'm going to miss my bus."

"I can drive you," he said, smoother than his goddamned shirt. "Did you want to finish reading those letters?"

"Now?"

"Yes, now."

"Here?" The night shift was coming in. We'd be in their way, and wouldn't they think it was weird that we didn't leave as soon as we clocked off?

Julian's gaze met mine. Something honest and intense flickered in those brown-and-amber eyes. "Well, we're not supposed to take any mail from the premises, and me asking you to my place would seem too straightforward and probably inappropriate, so yes. Here." He turned back to his office door. "No one uses my office. I know the night crew. They won't mind if we're here for a bit."

I hadn't really processed anything he said after asking me back to his place and ashamedly, with that deep voice and those eyes in that handsome face, I would have agreed to whatever he suggested.

Dazed and with a belly full of butterflies, I nodded. "Yes."

CHAPTER SEVEN

"DO you have a pen and paper I could use?"

I was sitting across from him again, his desk between us, trying not to bring up the fact he wanted to ask me back to his place.

Don't say anything, Malachi. Just let it go, play it cool.

It didn't mean anything. It certainly didn't mean what I wanted it to mean, that this sexy-AF grown-ass man doesn't want to rearrange my intestines . . .

Oh great. Now I was thinking about that.

For the love of the old gods, Malachi, don't bring it up.

"So, I wouldn't find it inappropriate if you asked me back to your place."

So glad you didn't just say that out loud. Real slick, idiot.

Julian slid a notepad and pen toward me, and he smiled, his eyes alight. I was going to have to google brown-coloured gemstones because holy hell, they needed a name.

And because my stupid brain was still stuck on having my intestines rearranged via my arse and just didn't know when to quit, I added, "And I have no problem with straightforward."

Julian seemed to chew on his tongue for a few seconds while he got his response in order. Or maybe he was waiting for me to keep blabbering. Or maybe he was joking before. And oh god, what if he was joking?

Soooo I kept blabbering on. "Unless you were joking, that is. In any case, I said what I said and I have zero regrets. I mean, I've already twice called you attractive, I said it right to your attractive face, so we both know I have no filter."

"You're nervous," he noted casually.

"I feel like I'm in trouble. Like I'm in the principal's office." I put my hand to my forehead. "Which is kinda hot, not gonna lie."

He laughed and shook his head. "Should we read the letters?"

The letters . . .

The letters?

He glanced at the pile of Dearest Milton James letters, amused.

"Oh right, yes, the letters. The sole reason we're still here. Yes, reading those would be a great idea."

Ignoring his smug smile, I took the next letter in the pile, opened it, took a deep breath and began to read.

Dearest Milton James

I've seen you these last three days and every time my heart falls more in love with you. Every day we've found a place to be alone, kissing, touching, holding hands.

Feeling how much you enjoyed being pressed against me set me on fire in ways I've never known. I long to touch you there, for you to touch me there.

Perhaps tomorrow I'll muster the courage to ask permission.

Your leaving looms like dark storm clouds on the horizon. I know its arrival is inevitable, yet I fear the turmoil it brings more with every passing breath.

I read the next part out loud.

"I cherish every moment with you, though every touch is bittersweet knowing they are numbered."

I looked up at Julian, who was watching my every reaction.

"I think reading this is going to kill me," I admitted. "Either heartbreak or sexual frustration. Whichever happens first, I guess. Maybe both together. At the same time."

Julian smiled. "Just keep reading."

The next letter told of how they'd had to take Milton's father's car to the next town to go see his grandparents before he left for the army. They'd also spent a day with his sister and walked along the railway tracks. There was no mention of asking permission to touch certain places and no mention of any kissing.

He'd missed it, and he selfishly cursed the sister for needing babysitting when they could have spent alone time doing better things.

The next letter made my heart race.

Dearest Milton James,

Finally, after two long days, we were alone again. Your sister was at her friend's place, your parents at work, and we had the house to ourselves. You wasted no time at all taking me straight to your room.

You fixed my nerves when you pushed me onto your bed and lay down beside me. I knew then you were as desperate as I was. The passion and the urgency in your touch, your kiss.

You took me to heaven with a few strokes of your hand.

Then I did the same to you.

Nothing had ever felt so right. The way you held onto me, the way you whispered my name, how you felt in my hand.

I will never forget what we shared that day.

I looked up at Julian. "This is very personal."

He nodded slowly.

"Thank you," I said. "For wanting to keep these letters private."

He smiled, his eyes soft. "I'm surprised they weren't destroyed or archived. And I'm grateful that you encouraged me to search for the rightful owner."

"I didn't really encourage you."

His smile became a smirk. "Just keep reading."

So I did.

The letter after that spoke of a job prospect in the town council offices. The guy who wrote the letters, whose name we still didn't know, his aunty was hoping to line up a desk job for him. He wasn't overly enthused for it but he said, and I quote, "It was better than some of their old classmates from school who had to move to get work in the quarries or on sheep farms."

So I began to make notes of all the little clues, hoping it would help paint a bigger picture.

The next letter said they almost got caught by Mr Killian behind his hardware store. They weren't really doing anything, maybe walking a little too close to each other, but it was a swift and bitter reminder that being together in that way, what they were, was not acceptable.

They both went home after that, each to their own place, sad and a little scared.

"'What I feel for you isn't wrong.'" I read the letter out loud, my voice soft. "'What we are when we're together isn't a sin. Love isn't a sin, Milton James. You tried to hide the shame in your eyes, but I saw it. I hated how such a thing could mar the light in your eyes.'"

I sighed, my heart heavy. "Bloody hell."

Julian was staring at something across his office that I couldn't see. Nothing physical, but a memory, a dark thought, a moment of uncertainty perhaps. "It feels personal to read his account of it, doesn't it? Intimate, somehow."

"Like we're invading something very private and deeply personal. He's baring his heart, writing all the things he couldn't say out loud."

He smiled sadly. "There's an innocence there too. First love and teenage hormones is like a poetic catastrophe. It almost always ends badly, doesn't it?"

I considered that for a second. "I dunno about badly. Probably. I think people grow and start on different paths, and that's not a bad thing. If they grow apart because of fundamental differences, then taking different paths is a good thing."

He made a thoughtful face. "That's very insightful."

I shrugged. "We don't feel that way at the time though. I mean, being a hormonal teen with a broken heart is apocalyptic. But in hindsight, could you imagine still being with your first love?"

His eyes met mine and I wondered briefly if I'd overstepped. I remembered Cherry telling me Julian had broken up with his long-term boyfriend a few years ago, and I immediately regretted asking the question.

But then Julian smiled. "God, no. I was fourteen, and I fell in love with Robbie Moss. He was my high school crush for two years. He loved cars and that was so cool, you know, to a fourteen-year-old boy. He had slicked-back hair and grease-stained hands, and I sat next to him in science. I let him copy my work because it meant he'd sit closer to me." Julian laughed at the memory. "But then I went on to years eleven and twelve, and he dropped out after year ten to be a mechanic. Which he got fired from not long after. And last I heard he and his brothers did time for illegal street drag racing and stripping down stolen cars."

"Nice."

"What about you?"

"My first love?" I sighed. "Alex from *McLeod's Daughters*. My older sister used to watch it and I was kinda young, so I didn't really understand what attraction was, but I knew I didn't care when the girls showed some skin. But when that guy was on-screen, shirtless and all hot and sweaty and dirty, lifting bales of hay . . ." I let out a breath. "Well, I knew which I preferred to look at."

Julian laughed. "You like the cowboys?"

"In real life? No. Not that I've met any real ones, to be

honest. Don't get many of those in Newtown. Get plenty of the wannabe cowboys, and I've seen enough leather chaps in my life. But my real first love was my best friend in high school."

"Really?"

"Yep. Ended tragically. And when I say tragically, I mean that I helplessly pined after him while he slept his way through three netball teams and the senior girls basket-ball team."

"Ouch."

"It was all rather awful, but I was going for the full teen-angst experience and he really helped with that."

He smiled. "Are you still friends?"

"Not really. We just drifted. You know how that is."

He studied me for a second. "I do, yes."

"Anyway, my best friend now is Moni and she's very much a lesbian, and we decided both of us being gay is much less complicated all 'round. Well, that, and our love of dumplings and our mutual dislike for the same people was a strong foundation. So basically, we bitched about the same cliquey circles, ate a lot of food, and now we've been best friends for years."

"She sounds fun." Julian smiled. "I have two best friends. I guess you'd call them that. Curtis and Mitch. We've been friends since uni. We were in the same dorm. Real life and adulthood keeps us busy now, but we play racquetball some Tuesday nights and catch up when we can. Usually for dinner and a few too many wines every so often."

"Racquetball? I never would have guessed that."

"Why, what did you think I would play?"

"I have no clue. Maybe lawn bowls. How old are you?"

His mouth fell open and I laughed. "I'm just kidding!

But I don't know . . . I hadn't thought of you playing any sport. Maybe something quieter than racquetball. Like swimming or tennis."

He inhaled deeply, somewhat amused from the look on his face. At least I hoped that's what it was. Then he looked at the letters in front of me. "How about we pack these up for tomorrow. I better get you home."

"Oh, sure," I said, carefully sliding a folded letter back into its envelope. "I didn't mean to offend you. Did I offend you? I'm sorry if I did."

"I'm not offended. I'm also not that old. How old do you think I am?"

I looked at him, horrified. "I absolutely will not answer that question. I know entrapment when I see it. I don't care how old you are. In fact, I like older guys. Never really explored the whole daddy concept before, but I'm not opposed. I have the whole twink vibe going on, whether I like it or not. Given I'm twenty-seven but I look young and I have weirdos legit disappointed when they find out I'm not sixteen. I mean, honestly, how many sixteen-year-old boys have the beginning of crow's feet." I pointed at the corner of my eye, desperately wishing my mouth would shut the fuck up.

Did I really just tell him I'd never explored the daddy scene? And that I'm a twink?

Fucking hell, Malachi.

I met his eyes, horrified. "I'm just going to take the liberty of pretending I never said any of that, and I'd really appreciate it if you didn't hear it either."

He chuckled, a deep throaty sound that stirred the butterflies in my belly. "I'm thirty-four, by the way. Not really a daddy concept, unless you were sixteen, which if you were, we wouldn't be having this conversation." He leaned in and inspected my face. "Though the crow's feet really are a dead giveaway that you're not sixteen."

I gasped, duly offended. I covered the sides of my eyes with my hands. "I do not have crow's feet."

He laughed louder this time, a genuine sound. "I'm just kidding. Payback for the lawn bowls comment."

I liked this side of him. Like, I really liked it. He was funny and flirty, and so god help me, he was sexy.

I sat back in my seat, and while I aimed for sultry, I had no delusions of grandeur that it was probably more of an I-have-indigestion look. "Thirty-four isn't old. And yes, while you might have a tinge of grey in your hair, you're not a silver fox. *Yet.* Maybe a baby silver fox. Is there a gay term for that? I'm not up to speed. But being a daddy is more of a mindset than an age, don't you think?"

He stared at me, unblinking, smouldering, filthy-sexy. It set my blood on fire and everything inside me tightened and yearned . . . I was half a second away from sprawling myself on his desk and telling him just to fuck me right here.

But then he looked away. "I should get you home."

"Yes, for sure," I agreed, both relieved and disappointed that he wasn't ripping my clothes off or ordering me to my knees. Okay, so more disappointed than relieved. But still . . .

Things were shifting between us. There was electricity, a spark just waiting to catch fire. I wasn't imagining it.

I just didn't know which one of us would be brave enough to light the match.

CHAPTER EIGHT

"WHAT DO you mean he dropped you home?" Moni
asked.

I changed my phone to my other ear so I could shovel
some food in my mouth. "I mean, he just dropped me
home."

"It's disgusting that I can actually understand you while
you talk with a mouthful of food."

I finished chewing and swallowed. "Sorry."

"Did he kiss you?"

My fork stopped halfway to my mouth. "No. God. I
don't think we're there yet."

"But you want to be . . ."

"He is so fine," I hummed. "One hundred per cent not
my type but perfect in every way."

"Malachi, your type, until now, has been the emotion-
ally unavailable, brain-dead muscle guys who want nothing
but a quick fuck. I'm glad this guy is not your type. Nothing
would make me happier if you started dating a guy who was
the opposite of your type."

"I don't think we'll be dating. I mean, we work together and he's my boss, technically.

"But you want to."

"I want him to do unspeakable things—"

"Could you perhaps stop eating?"

"I'm starving."

"So what about the letters?"

"I'll finish reading them tomorrow," I said, this time without the mouthful of food.

"Promise you'll give me an update."

"Promise."

"Go finish your dinner."

"I will, thanks."

"Are we still on for Saturday night?"

"Yes. Unless I have a better offer for a deep dicking, then . . . well, you understand."

She snorted. "I'll keep my fingers crossed for you. Good luck with the sexy boss-man."

"Uh, thanks."

"And Malachi?"

"Yes?"

"If things do go the way you want them to—and he does sound interested, from what you've told me—then you need to have a conversation about work and where you both stand with that."

I refrained from sighing. "I know."

"Love you."

"Love you too."

We disconnected at the same time and I finished shovelling in my veggie lasagne, happy with . . . well, with everything. With my job, with Julian.

I'd hoped like crazy he might have said something on the car ride home or even asked any kind of personal question like 'Are you seeing anyone?' or 'Do you want to invite me up to your flat where I can fuck you into the mattress?' . . . you know, those kinds of questions.

But he never said anything like that.

Maybe it was the confined space of his car that would have made it super awkward if I turned him down, or maybe the fun and flirty jokes were just a joke. Maybe he was smart enough to realise that nothing could happen between us and knew better than to play a game where we both lost.

Stop overthinking it, Malachi.

Easier said than done. Actually, overthinking and making mountains out of molehills were the two things I did best.

But I told myself to let it go. *Take each day as it comes, enjoy your work, Malachi, enjoy working on the letters with Julian, enjoy having fun and flirty conversations for the sake of being fun and flirty and nothing else.*

Easy peasy.

And absolutely one hundred per cent go to bed and watch some porn while thinking of Julian and orgasm so hard you almost black out.

That was the plan.

And that was exactly what I did.

I WAS EXCITED for work the next day. I arrived a little early, put my lunch in the breakroom fridge, and made my first coffee. Paul was already there, flipping casually through his newspaper while Theo chatted away at him about last night's episode of *Survivor*. Paul didn't seem to be listening. Theo didn't appear to realise or care.

I said a quick hello but stirred my coffee at the counter for an eternity to avoid having to join in their conversation and was thankfully spared when Cherry walked in. She wore black and pink today and smiled at me like a gorgeous goth Bratz doll.

"Morning," she said quietly, her eyes bright. "So what happened between you and Julian last night?"

I almost spat out my first sip. "What? Nothing. Why?"

She took her cup from the cupboard, smiling like she knew some delicious secret. "Because he's wearing blue."

I blinked. "What?"

"Mr Brown, Mr Beige, Mr Every Shade of Taupe That Exists is wearing blue."

"Blue?"

Cherry nodded and poured boiling water into her cup, the teabag dangling precariously over the side. "I would say it's a pale sky blue or even a powder blue. I'm not sure. And his pants are—" She met my eyes. "—navy."

I swallowed. "He's wearing blue."

She nodded again. "Obviously something cosmic happened to him, and you two stayed late last night. I know you think he's handsome, and I've seen him look at you."

My eyeballs almost popped out of my sockets like grapes. "I . . . uh . . . what? No I don't, and he doesn't . . . I mean, does he? Look at me . . .?"

She smirked. "Every time he comes out of his office he looks at your desk first. He looks for *you* first."

I whispered. "He does not."

She squinted at me. "Your smile is a little frightening. Could you turn the wattage down a bit? I have sensitive retinas."

I held my cup up to cover my mouth. "Sorry. But, oh my god, is he wearing blue?"

And sure as hell, right then, the break room door opened and Mr Blue walked in.

Holy fucking hell.

Was that shirt a little more fitted than his brown ones?

Cherry nudged me and I closed my mouth. Paul stared, noticing the colour change as well, but Theo was oblivious, still talking about immunity tikis or some such rubbish.

"Morning," Julian said. The tips of his ears were tinged pink. He was uncertain or nervous, but there were no other tells. He strode in, looking confident as ever even if I knew his ears were a giveaway to the contrary. He made his coffee, strong and black, and smiled as he sipped it.

"Is that powder blue or summer periwinkle?" I asked.

He met my gaze. He had to know I was going to bring it up. May as well just get it out of the way. "It's just blue."

I nodded slowly. "It's very nice."

"Nice?"

"I was going to say dapper but thought I'd gay it down a bit. And just so you know, nothing is *just* blue. There has to be a gay qualifier. It's the law."

"And is summer periwinkle a gay qualifier?"

I nodded, because, uh, hello. Of course it was. Did he not hear himself just now?

He smiled as he swallowed his coffee. His brown eyes glittered directly at me. "I'll keep that in mind."

He nodded to the others as he walked out, and I watched the glory that was his arse in those navy pants. Cherry nudged me again. "Christ," she breathed, pulling at the collar of her black-and-pink argyle sweater. "Could you two tone it down a bit? Or go into his office and lock the door for a while?"

I shot her a look. "What?"

"The testosterone and pheromones are stifling."

I rolled my eyes but couldn't help but smile. I turned to her so Paul couldn't see my face. "He looks fucking hot today."

"Sure nothing happened between you last night?"

"Nothing, I swear. We stayed here for an hour or so, then he drove me home."

Cherry stared. And I mean stared. "And you expect me to believe that nothing happened?"

"It didn't."

"What were you doing here for an hour by yourselves?"

Shit. "We were . . ."

Now here's the thing. This wasn't supposed to be public, but not hidden either. I trusted Cherry, and the alternative was her assuming Julian and I had some crazy desk sex, which wasn't right. I mean, it was hot. But it was, unfortunately, not true.

"You know those really old letters in his office that have been here since the seventies?"

Cherry nodded once.

"We're trying to find the owner or the recipient. Which-ever one we can find." Her eyes grew wide with excitement so I put my hand up. "We're doing it on the quiet," I whispered. "Julian didn't want anyone else to know, so please don't breathe a word of it to anyone. The letters are very . . . personal."

"You've read them?"

"I'm about halfway through."

"And?"

"And I haven't found much. I'm hoping he divulges more in the next few letters. I'm making notes of any clues I can find."

"He?"

"The man who wrote them. To another man. Before he went off to the Vietnam War."

"Oh my god." She sipped her tea, eyes wide. "Are they explicit?"

"Not really by today's standard, but I'd imagine back in the seventies in small-town Australia, yes. Anything sexual he writes is more poetic than erotic."

"You know it's a small town?"

I nodded. "Can guess as much. I don't know where yet though."

Denise walked in then. "Mornin'," she said loud and hoarse as she began making herself a coffee. "Hope you got some caffeine into ya because today's haul is huge. Dunno why it is, but I just lifted a fuckton of crates off the truck."

Right, then. Morning chat time was over. Paul and Theo stood up and washed their cups, Cherry tipped the rest of her tea down the sink, and I looked at the last mouthful of cold coffee in my cup and decided to do the same. Everyone rushed out to the floor to begin their day.

Cherry and I grabbed our first crate together. "Once you get all your notes in order, if you need any help, let me know," she said quietly.

"I will, thanks."

Denise wasn't kidding when she said there was a lot of incoming mail today. We were basically running all day. Parcels, packages, letters, boxes, satchels. Even Julian left his accounts and reports and emptied a cage or two.

I spied his gorgeous navy-and-summer-periwinkle-wearing self as he pushed a cart through the aisles a few times. Apparently, according to Cherry, he'd help whenever needed, and he did without having to be asked. He took one look at the incoming inventory and just helped out, and I really liked that about him.

But he was wearing blue today, not brown, for the first time in as long as Cherry had worked here. There had to be a reason. There just had to be. And I tried not to overthink it or imagine I had any part in that, because why would I?

Then some godawful sinking horrible realisation occurred to me in the middle of aisle D-E. What if there was another reason?

What if there was another guy? What if he had a new man that no one knew about?

I held a parcel of new sports socks that had somehow lost its address label and I started to feel a little hot and cold all over.

Fuckity fuck.

What if Julian was seeing someone that wasn't me?

Should I be surprised? No. Should I be heartbroken that Mr Sexy who I'd been fantasising about for weeks didn't think of me the way I thought of him?

"You okay?" a deep voice asked behind me.

I startled, tossing the parcel of socks across the aisle. "Oh shit!"

Julian picked it up and handed it to me. "Everything okay?"

"Oh yeah, sure. Sure, why wouldn't I be? I mean it doesn't matter if you're seeing someone. Why would it matter? It's completely fine, and admittedly, all rather delusional that I would think you might have liked me. I mean, let's be real. I'm not your type. I'm not anyone's type, just between you and me. A little too loud and sunshiny for most people, which is cool. That's just who I am; I won't apologise. But I'm glad you're wearing blue today. Summer periwinkle is a fabulous colour. I might go back to blue." I pulled at the still-purple streak in my black hair. "Although I was thinking green next time, but it's a fine line between an amazing apple green and a zombie-chlorine green. But when it's done right, it looks great."

Julian blinked and shook his head, a little confused. "Um, that was a lot of information. I'm not sure where I should start . . ."

I took a step backwards, bumping into my cart. "Sorry. You know, nervous rambling, grandmaster level. Seldom few achieve it."

Julian put his hand on my arm. He looked two parts concerned, four parts amused, a billion parts sexy as fuck.

I never was any good at maths.

"Malachi, are you okay?"

His deep and low voice knocked me out of my stupor. I nodded. "Yep. Sure am. Thank you for asking. I hope you and your new boyfriend are very happy together."

He chuckled. "What are you talking about?"

Was he not here for my Hamlet-worthy soliloquy?

"Uh, I probably should have asked this before. Not that it's any of my business to be honest. But . . ." Gawwwwwd. "You know what? It's not any of my business. And if you wanted me to know, you would have told me and the fact you haven't is all I need to know." I put the parcel of socks on the shelf and scanned it, marking it as logged. "I'm fine, Julian. Thank you for asking, but I have a lot of work to get done. I'm happy to keep working on the Dearest Milton James letters though." I checked my watch. I'd missed lunch. "Oh. Well, after work again is fine—"

"I like working on the floor," he said, completely off-topic. It kinda startled me. "I should do it more often. Cataloguing and searching, finding someone's lost letter or parcel. It's rewarding."

Okay then. And I thought my randomness was weird. "It is. I actually really like my job. I like it more each day."

"I'm not seeing anyone," he said, his voice barely above a whisper. "Though this is probably a conversation best had somewhere that isn't here." He picked up a box from his cart. "I better keep going with these. This here box contains a soccer field for a fish tank so your goldfish can play soccer. Quality, life-changing stuff."

"Nemo's going to be so disappointed that it was never delivered," I replied. I was about to suggest he check the address 42 Wallaby Way but thankfully my brain stopped me.

Julian smiled as he walked off, and I had to take a second to catch my breath. He was single. He told me he was single. And he told me we should be talking about this kind of stuff not at work, which meant he did want to talk about this kind of stuff, just not here.

He wanted to talk about him not seeing anyone and me saying I wanted him to like me. And he said all this while smiling and not with a horrified look of disgust.

I felt giddy.

I did manage a very late lunch, which I ate at my desk while searching up names and addresses. I sent a few parcels on to their rightful owners and went back to shelving the ones I couldn't win.

Five o'clock couldn't come around quick enough and everyone left pretty much on time while I scrambled to pack up and log out without looking too excited. "Have fun," Cherry said, glancing pointedly at Julian's door.

I tried to roll my eyes but was also trying not to smile, and as it turned out, I could only do one at a time. She laughed as she walked out with a wave over her shoulder.

But when I knocked on Julian's door, he was standing at his desk, packing up, his computer screen off.

"Oh," I said. No point in trying to hide my disappointment. "I just assumed we'd be working on the letters again and I missed a chance at lunch. It's fine if you don't want to." Then something occurred to me. "Shit. I'll miss the bus."

"Malachi, wait," he said, stopping me from making a start for the front door. He waited until I gave him my full attention. He was nervous again, the tips of ears pink, and he fidgeted with his satchel on his desk. "Don't worry about the bus. I can drive you."

"Are you sure? Because if I run . . ." I cringed. "Actually, if I do run, I would formally request you not watch because if you've ever seen a newborn giraffe try and use its legs—"

He met my eyes and smiled. "I wanted to work on the letters again."

"Oh." Okay, I was confused . . .

"I wondered if you wanted to work on them somewhere else? Somewhere not here?"

My belly tightened. "Oh?" That sounded auspiciously like maybe a date? That giddiness was back. "I thought we couldn't take any mail or product from the premises."

Julian straightened a little. "Any mail that comes through the system isn't to be taken off the premises, that's true. But the Milton James letters haven't been in the system. Not for about thirty years."

"You mean, they just live here without record?"

He nodded. "Since well before I started."

"So, you want me to read them somewhere else?" Then I remembered something. "Hang on a minute. You told me we had to read them here."

He met my eyes and swallowed. "I thought it would be best."

"But now?"

He looked down at his satchel, played with the buckle,

and let out a quiet laugh. "Okay, here's the deal. I'm just going to be completely honest with you."

"Okaaaay."

"I like you." He put his hand up quickly, palm forward. "Not in a weird way. I just think you're . . . I don't know. Maybe this is weird. You said earlier that you're sunshiny and loud, and that's true. I've been . . ." He made a face. "I kind of shut myself off for a long time and I didn't realise I missed the sunshiny, loud type of people until you walked in with your sunshine-lemon sweater." He gestured to my actual sweater.

I tried not to be offended. "Uh, this is lemon-sorbet yellow."

He smiled, the eye-crinkling kind. "Sorry. Lemon-sorbet yellow. The gay qualifiers . . . I'm so far behind."

"I can give lessons."

He smiled again, a little crooked this time, but then it faded away. "I tried to not like you." He stared into my eyes then. "But after I drove you home and you said you found me attractive, I thought maybe some professional distance would be appropriate."

I remembered that. "You didn't speak to me for a few days. I wondered if I'd done something wrong. I mean, apart from saying you were attractive. To your face."

Julian shook his head slowly, almost smiling. "You didn't do anything wrong. Sorry if I confused you. I didn't mean to. I was just trying to steady myself. I meant what I said about not realising how much I'd missed . . . being happy." He ran his hand through his hair and blew out a breath. "It was a bit of a wake-up call."

"Is that . . . does that explain the wardrobe change?"

He looked down at what he was wearing and let out a laugh. "Ah, not really. Maybe. I do own other colours. I just wore the same clothes to work, like a uniform. And . . . someone once told me brown suited me. I got stuck wearing it, every day, and I don't know why."

"Brown does suit you. It matches your eyes."

Julian's smile turned sad and he nodded.

"But the blue is smoking hot," I added. This conversation was wholly weird and skirting well into personal territory, so I was unsure where to tread. "And the fitted shirt. I was liking the brown until you showed up in that shirt."

I swear he blushed. "I was going to go with the white one."

"Classic white or fresh-linen white?"

"Fresh-linen white, for sure."

"You have no clue and just repeated what I said."

He chuckled. "Correct."

"You could have made one up."

"Such as?"

"Anything. Wildflower white, snow dream, or winter white."

"I lack both the imagination and the quick wit for that. And you'd have known for sure anyway." His eyes drew down to my sweater. "Is that really lemon sorbet? Or did you make that up?"

I found myself smiling at him. "Oh, it's real. I've been known to purchase things because of their pretty names. How can you not buy a sweater called lemon sorbet?"

He met my eyes and for a long moment, he didn't look away. "So, these letters . . . Did you want to go to a restaurant or bar?"

"I would, normally, yes. But am I going to cry reading the rest of the letters? Julian, there's a really good chance I'm going to snot-sob, so is being in public a good idea? The other customers will probably assume you're breaking up with me and you'll get death glares from everyone and we'll be TikTok famous and it will be a whole ordeal . . . though I might get free pity-drinks, so it might not be a terrible plan. We could make it work."

He chuckled again. "We could get some takeout dinner and go to the park at the end of your street."

I made a face. As sweet as that sounded, it wasn't a great idea. "We could. As long as the sun's still out. Once it gets dark, it gets sketchy as hell, and I'm far too pretty to be thrown into the Hunger Games."

He grinned. "Noted."

"We can go back to my place if you want?" I asked without really thinking that through. "I mean, not for anything other than takeout food and reading these letters, and so I can blubber like Judy Blume in the privacy of my own flat."

Julian stared at me, smiling, but there was definitely some conflict going on in those eyes. "Are you sure?"

I nodded, because I was sure. Now that I'd asked, I wanted him to come back to my place. I wanted to spend time with him outside of work, and my place was where I was most comfortable. "I'm not suggesting anything or implying anything. And it's not an invitation for anything else. We're not dating, after all, and I'm not that kind of guy."

If Moni heard those words tumble out of my mouth, she would have died laughing.

The corner of Julian's mouth quirked upwards. "Noted."

THE DRIVE back to my place was kinda quiet. Nervous and excited and trying not to show it, I decided to talk about dinner options that we could order in. Though it's likely he knew I was nervous because I might have talked about the adobo at my favourite Filipino restaurant for ten minutes straight, with a very honourable mention to the dumplings from the corner noodle bar.

Julian knew I was prone to ramble when nervous and thankfully he didn't seem to mind. He even smiled and looked at me occasionally as though he found me adorable.

Which of course made me more nervous.

He was coming back to my place. There was a possibility that we could kiss or make out or, as I was trying very hard not to think about, we could end up in bed.

See, I have the best of intentions. It's just my willpower that's lacking.

But I had to be strong.

I couldn't just be falling into bed with my boss on a whim.

I mean, I *could* . . . but I probably shouldn't.

He said he liked me. In his office, that's what he said. He said I was the sunshine he didn't know he was missing, and that was possibly the nicest thing anyone has ever said to me.

"You sure you're okay with this? Because we can try to read the letters at lunchtime tomorrow if we're not so busy."

I glanced at Julian, then outside my window. I hadn't even realised we were in my street, let alone parked. "Yes, of course. Sorry, I was just thinking . . ." I shook my head and lifted my bag onto my lap. "Let's get inside and I can order us something. I'm starving."

Not that I was actually starving, but ordering the food, waiting for the delivery person, then eating the food was a whole lot of time where I wouldn't be tempted to find out how Julian felt against me, or what he tasted like, or how he kissed . . .

Yes, food was a great idea.

I fumbled a little getting out of his car and tried to play it cool as he followed me up to my flat. I was always a tidy person; I lived by myself, so my flat was respectable for company. "Come in."

I led him into the small living room which opened up to the old kitchen. I put my bag on the retro laminate table. "Can I get you a drink?" I opened my fridge. "I have . . . water, lemon mineral water, and Canadian Club cans. Or tea and coffee."

"Uh, lemon mineral water would be great, thanks." He looked around, smiling. "Your place is very . . . you."

I laughed and conceded a nod. There was a mismatch of funky coloured cushions and the record-cover artwork on the walls. "Thanks. Moni and I go thrifting all the time. Her house looks more like an op-shop, where I like to think I make more refined and select purchases. Don't tell her I said that."

I handed him his drink, grabbed the pile of takeaway menus, and went to my couch. "You can pick. I'm easy."

He wanted the adobo I'd raved about, so once that was ordered, Julian pulled his satchel over and took out the letters.

Oh yes, the letters . . .

What he was here for.

I got up and collected the box of tissues off the kitchen bench and went back, sitting on the floor this time, leaning against the couch. "I'm ready for all the tears now."

Julian smiled as he handed the letters over to me. "They're not that bad."

"Well, I cry if there's an ad with a dog in it. It doesn't have to die or anything. It just has to be in it, so . . ."

Julian chuckled. "The ads aren't so bad for me. But if a dog dies in a movie or a book? I will cry then."

I gasped. "Oh my god. In a movie? No one is forgiven. I mean, no one. That movie *Hachi*, with Richard Gere. Well, Richard Gere is now dead to me. The screenwriters? The entire supporting cast? Dead to me. The most unfortunate people who sat beside me in the movie theatre and had to hear me sob? They're dead to me. Every single person."

Julian laughed. "So, no suggesting we watch *Marley and Me* over dinner."

I gawped at him. "Is that some kind of litmus test because—"

He put his hand up. "Just kidding."

"I would rather watch the *Titanic* a dozen times and cheerfully see Jack turned into a popsicle every single time."

He grinned but then made a face. "I wonder if there were any dogs on the Titanic."

My mouth fell open. "Why would you say such a thing?" I put my hand to my forehead. "God, I bet there was. Why does no one talk about these things? I'm never watching the Titanic again."

Julian nodded slowly, smiling. After a while, he said, "There was room on that floating door for Jack."

"Oh my god, I know, right? Bitch just let him die like that."

Julian laughed again and sipped his drink. He looked so casual and relaxed, just chilling at my place, like he'd done this a thousand times, like he belonged here.

It was a comforting thought before I realised it was all in my head. I wanted him to relax and chill at my place as though he belonged.

Wishful thinking was a dangerous game.

With a bit of a start, I remembered the letter I was holding and began to read it.

Dearest Milton James,

Holding your hand is a dream, even if no one can see. I know what it feels like. I have committed it to memory. Kissing you is what heaven must feel like.

I'll never tire of it. Each time it's a thrill I never dreamed possible.

The way you smile at me, the way your hand caresses my face, how you feel against me . . .

"Oh, dear god," I mumbled, fanning my face. "He sure does have a way with words."

I was beginning to think I might need those tissues for something other than tears.

Julian chuckled. "It's rather poetic."

"Poetic and hot."

I handed it to him so he could re-read, and I picked up the next letter. It was no less beautiful.

Dearest Milton James,

I told my Aunt Kath I'd rather not take the job she was trying to line up for me. I want to go to Sydney for university. Something I wouldn't perhaps have considered if you weren't leaving.

I wanted to be where you are, but that can't happen now.

Most people think me foolish for wanting to become a teacher. But not you. You told me to chase my dream, to follow my heart.

I told you my heart was leaving to join the army, and you kissed me and held me so tight.

You told me your heart would stay with me no matter where in this world we are.

I love you, Milton James.

One day I'll say those words to you, using your real name.

One day.

———————————————————————

I sighed and folded the letter gently. I scribbled down a few notes. "So romantic."

Julian looked over at me then. "Which one are you up to?"

I handed it to him and gave him a few seconds to read it. "But not just that one. It's all of them, I mean. The whole thing. Writing love letters to the man you love but knowing he'll never read them. Addressing them incorrectly, to a name that's not his lover's real name, no stamp. But still needing his words to be out in the universe somewhere."

I sighed again just as the intercom buzzed. "That'll be dinner," I said, and sure enough, five minutes later we were sat on the floor, using the couch as a backrest, the letters tucked away so I didn't spill the contents all over them. We had our legs stretched out, crossed at the ankles.

Julian was a delicate eater. Small, polite bites, but he tilted his head to the side every so often in a cute little dance and hummed his approval. At first I thought I imagined the groan-like sounds, but no, it was him.

"Good?" I asked.

"Mm." He swallowed his mouthful. "It's wonderful. Thank you for suggesting it."

"You can get the next one," I said, half joking, half not. I mean, I had paid this time. Not that I was one to keep score, but if it meant a second date . . .

Julian smiled, his brown eyes glittering. "Deal."

"I don't always sit on the floor, you know," I said, waving my fork at the table.

"It's fun though," he said.

"Fun? Just wait until you try and stand up."

He chuckled. "It's been a while since I ate dinner sitting on the floor."

"You don't bring crazy-hot dates back to your place and make them sit on the floor to eat? What kind of sensible guy are you?"

He smirked as he chewed, and I wondered if I'd crossed a line. "A sensibly kind of boring one."

"Boring? I doubt that."

He made a face as he stabbed more of his dinner with his fork. "Boring and sensible. That's actually pretty accurate."

"You say that like it's a bad thing. Those two qualities aren't bad." I put my takeout container down, too full to eat another bite. "And boring and sensible by whose definition?"

"My ex."

Oh.

"He said that to you?"

"Yes, he did."

"Well, first of all, fuck him for saying that. How dare he. And second, being quiet or reserved, or introverted or reflective, isn't boring and sensible. Being any or all of those things is a wonderful trait. Wanting to stay in and watch a movie or read a book, or whatever, is just as valid as going clubbing. And to be honest, I'd prefer the kind of guy who'd rather talk over dinner than go out all the time any day."

He laughed. "Thank you for saying that. But honestly, my ex was probably right. I never wanted to—"

"Hey. If you didn't want to do something and he resented you for that, then he was not the right person for you."

Julian met my eyes, and after a few seconds, he looked away. "You're pretty smart."

"And cute."

He laughed again. "I didn't mean to drag our conversation down, sorry. The whole ex thing was a few years ago and I *am* over it. But I did get . . . stagnant, or boring. I just forgot to look up every now and again."

"Until I walked in wearing Colour-Pop-blue boots and a matching fancy tie."

"And your matching hair." He laughed again. "I don't want you to think I'm pinning my whole outlook on you turning up, because I'm not. It was just a good reminder."

Wow.

Okay, so holy shit.

I tried not to panic. He just said, basically, that meeting me reminded him to live. How could I not feel giddy and floaty? "Reminders are good." My voice came out all breathy and I sounded like a really bad impersonation of Marilyn Monroe. I cleared my throat. "So, your ex . . ."

"He cheated on me and then blamed me for it," Julian replied, very matter of factly. "It wasn't the first time either, apparently."

"Oh man, I'm so sorry."

"It kind of messed me up for a bit, not gonna lie. I had our whole lives planned out like a fool."

"No, he was the fool."

Julian smiled at me, then shook his head. "I have no idea why I'm telling you all this."

"It's obvious," I declared. "You're telling me all this so we can make a voodoo doll of him and make him suffer." Oh my god, this was possibly my best idea ever. "We could follow him, and when he tries to pick up some unfortunate unsuspecting guy, we can just give him a little tap in the back of the head or stick a pin in his dick, and we'll be watching from across the bar and we can laugh and laugh."

Julian chuckled. "I don't think we need to do that."

"Ooh, we could soak the voodoo doll in laxatives. That would be an experiment for the ages."

He cracked up, and it was so beautiful. His deep voice, the little crease lines at the corner of his eyes, his neck, his throat, his smile, and those lips . . .

"Remind me never to piss you off," he said.

"I wouldn't do it for real. But it's nice to imagine." I sighed. "I'm sorry he did that. You deserve better."

"I know I do. Now. It took me a while to realise that. I swore off men for a long time."

"Oh, honey, I swear off men every weekend."

He smiled at that. "So what about you?" he hedged. "What horrible ex-boyfriend stories do you have?"

"Well, I've never had a real boyfriend," I admitted. He couldn't hide his shock. "I mean, I've had boyfriends and guys I've dated for a few weeks or months, but none that I had my life planned out with."

He studied my face and settled on my eyes. "Have you ever been in love?"

"Every Friday night," I replied with a laugh. "Just kidding. Sure I have, I think. I loved all the guys I've dated and called a boyfriend, but not *love* love. I loved being with them, or loved something about them, or loved that they made me laugh, or loved what they did to me in the bedroom, but as for real love? I don't know." I felt rather foolish for admitting this. "I love everything though. Those album covers on the wall? I love them. These lilac shoes? I love them. My neighbour in the next flat has a cat that likes to sleep on my balcony. I would die for that cat. His name is Buster Jones and I love him. I sneak him some diced ham or chicken every night, but it's our little secret. My friend Moni has a leather jacket that is tangerine orange and I love it so much. I've begged her for it but she refuses. The best she would do is bequeath it to me in her will. I told her not to give me a reason to kill her, but she just laughed and said I could never kill her because I have the upper body strength of wet paper." I shrugged. "I mean, she's not wrong, but—"

"Why are you nervous?"

"Because I've never been in *love* love, and you're sitting really close and your eyes are so pretty. They're like fire agate. I had to google that, just so you know. And you keep looking at me like you might want to kiss me and I wouldn't say no, even though you're technically my boss and I told Moni all about you and she made me promise that we would talk about work boundaries before I let anything happen and—"

He looked at my lips and slow blinked, his gaze trailing slowly back up to my eyes.

Had I stopped talking or was my heart thumping in my ears and I just couldn't hear?

He licked his lips.

Every cell in my body felt alive, electric, buzzing and wanting more. And if he leaned in and kissed me right then,

I would have straddled his lap and made short work of us both.

I was just about to do that anyway when he let out a shaky breath and seemed to break out of whatever trance he was in.

"Yeah," he said, rough and husky. "We should probably talk."

CHAPTER NINE

"TALKING IS A GOOD IDEA," I said. "So is climbing you like a tree and asking you to take me to bed, but yes, talking probably is better. I seem to do a lot of that, so perhaps you should go first?"

Christ, Malachi, just stop talking.

Julian chuckled and ran his hand through his hair. We were still sitting on the floor, leaning against the couch. "I think the work-boundary conversation is a good place to start," he said.

I nodded, stupidly. Pretty sure he could have said that purple flying aliens were coming to take over the world and I would have nodded and agreed.

"I like you, Malachi," he said, his cheeks a lovely warm pink. "I tried not to like you as anything more than a colleague but . . ." He smiled with a shrug. "That didn't work out. I'm going to be straight-up with you, no pretences or anything, and just tell you that I would like to see you outside of work. I haven't been interested in seeing anyone, let alone dating, for a long time. But then you walked into my office and it was like a lightbulb went on."

Holy shit.

He was just putting all this out there, no hedging, no dancing around, just straight-up saying what he wanted.

And what he wanted was me.

Christ, he could just voice his feelings, his wants and whatever like a freaking grown-up, and all I could do was nod.

So I nodded.

He smiled and I eventually found my voice. "I would like that. To see you outside of work, that is. Like we are right now."

His smile grew wider, relieved, happy.

Until I added, "But work . . ."

And his smile stumbled. "It complicates matters, I know."

"I really like my job. And I've never liked a job before. I've never had a job I actually look forward to going to, and I want to keep it."

He nodded. "I understand."

"That doesn't mean I don't *not* want to see you either. I . . ." I could only shrug. "I don't know what it means. That was a lot of negatives. Did one cancel the other out? I'm not sure but you know what I mean."

Julian gave me a sad smile. "I'm glad you like your job. When you first started, you weren't sure you'd stay."

"I was certain I wouldn't. You just kinda smiled like you knew I'd fit in."

"I was sure you would. Your father didn't think you'd last."

"My father . . . Actually, I've probably never given my father reason to think I would last in any job." I smiled at that. "He was more surprised than me when I told him I wanted to stay. And honestly, it was very embarrassing to have my father take me to see you. I felt like I was back in my high school principal's office after another detention."

"You got detention? I can't imagine that."

Oooh, sarcasm. I liked it. He was allowing me to see more of his real self. "Teachers loved me. Sometimes. As long as I didn't have to speak up for any wrongs or social injustices or defend victims of bullying. Then we got along just fine."

He met my eyes. "Have you always stuck up for the little guy? After all, you did wear a skirt to prove a point about unfair dress codes."

"Always. And I think as crazy as I drove my parents with my ability to change jobs like I changed my hair, they've always been proud of what I stand up for. If someone was in trouble or if they needed help or were too afraid to speak up, I'd do it for them. My dad can't be too mad when I'm exercising the principles he drilled into me."

"Even if it bites him in the arse."

"Especially then."

He sipped his drink. "It's an admirable quality."

I smirked. "My mouth has gotten me into a lot of trouble."

His eyes went to my lips and he stared. "I can see why."

Well, holy shit.

That was very blatant, and the static between us kicked up a notch. It was clear there was something between us, but what could we do about it? This whole conversation with him was going around in circles. "So how do we . . . do we even try to see each other? I don't even know what I'm asking for."

Julian licked his lips and his attention went to his hands resting on his lap. "There's no corporate policy for our office that prohibits any such relationships," he said. "So that's one thing, I guess."

"But then there's the power exchange," I added. "You know, if we did start something and then you realised that I'm a whole lot more sunshine than you bargained for, then you could fire me."

He put his hand to his chest. "I wouldn't . . ." Then he made a face. "But I could. I see your point, sorry."

"And it's not just that," I said. "What if the others think you're more lenient on me or more unfair to them, or I don't know . . . anything to make them think I have an advantage because you and I have the best sex life ever and they're all jealous."

He chuckled at that, but then he sighed. "I don't know. It's complicated."

"It is."

"I don't know what the answer is."

Fuck.

"I don't either. But I'm glad we talked."

"Same, Malachi. I . . ."

"You what?"

He shook his head. "Nothing. I don't know what I was going to say. I . . . wish I knew. The more we talk, the more I wish. But you're right. We need to be professional, and you don't want to lose your job, I don't want to lose mine. I really love our little group of . . ."

"Misfits?"

Julian chuckled and nodded. "Yeah. I'm glad you're enjoying your work and I don't want to jeopardise that."

"It doesn't mean we can't still hang out," I said, quelling my disappointment that whatever was budding between us would end right here before it even had a chance to bloom.

"We can still do dinner and watch movies or go to art museums with charcoal drawings of naked men."

He smiled and gave a nod, though he seemed as disappointed as I felt. "Sounds good."

"So these letters," I said, changing subjects and trying to lift the mood. "I don't have many to go."

Julian nodded. "Just one thing first."

I held my breath. "Sure."

"Can we sit on the couch? My arse is numb."

I burst out laughing. "Yes, of course."

"How about you keep reading, and I'll clean all this up." He'd already picked up our takeout containers and took them to the kitchen, so there wasn't any real point in arguing that he was a guest and shouldn't be cleaning up.

The next letter was mostly mentions of family and what was going on in town and, of course, the looming departure for the army. There was a definite sense of their ending and a goodbye that was getting closer every day.

I made a few notes from details I wasn't sure meant anything. "Uh, there's a cat at your balcony door," Julian said.

"Oh, that's Buster Jones. Can you let him in, please?"

He opened the door and Buster Jones walked in, circled around and in between Julian's feet, meowing his discontent rather loudly. Julian looked at me, panicked. "He's very vocal. Is he mad at me?"

"There's some diced ham in the fridge. Or chicken. Whatever's in there. If you could just give him a little bit, that'd be great. There's an old olive container. I use that to feed him in."

"I can't believe you feed your neighbour's cat," he said, but he served up some diced deli ham. He put the container down on the ground, Buster pounced on it, and Julian grinned at me. "He likes it."

"He loves it. He usually thanks me with a cuddle."

And sure enough, as soon as Buster finished his little snack, he trotted over to me on the couch, jumped up, and gave me a purry head bump. He sat with me for a while before sprawling himself out on the carpet in front of the TV. I smiled and took out the next letter.

It was a little more interesting than the last.

Dearest Milton James,

You're leaving in three days and my heart isn't ready to break. Your family barbeque was nice for you, seeing your cousins before you leave made you happy. Even though I selfishly wanted every minute with you alone.

I know you need time with them too, so I take comfort in seeing you smile.

I finally plucked up the courage to ask you to be with me, to have me the way a man might have a woman. I was so scared. I thought you'd be horrified, that you'd say no and turn me away.

But you said you wanted nothing in the world more.

I could feel the honesty in your touch, the sincerity in your kiss.

"Oh god, this is too much," I breathed. "'I could feel the honesty in your touch.' Christ, who says that?"

Julian had come back to the sofa and was sitting beside me. "It's beautiful, isn't it?"

I held up the letter. "This is romance. Not like Rose who let Jack drown when there was room on the door. That's not romance. That's second-degree homicide. *This* is romance."

Julian smiled. "Negligent homicide, even."

I nodded. He got it. He understood the outrage. "Right?" I sighed. "Now I'm mad."

I attempted to stuff the letter back in its envelope but he took it off me. "Let me do that for you."

Probably a good idea. I was likely to damage it with my stabby hands. "Next letter better not piss me off. I feel like writing a letter to James Cameron. Fucking Jack and Rose. Ugh. Like Romeo and Juliet. Honestly. They all end up dead."

I shot a look to Julian, holding the next letter to my chest. "Oh my god, these two better not end up dead. Julian, I'll never forgive you if you make me read this and they die. You said he didn't die."

"He doesn't." Then he made a face. "In these letters he doesn't. But I can't guarantee they're both still alive now."

I stared at him. "Oh god. Why did you say that?"

Julian reached over and gave my hand a squeeze. "Just keep reading."

I sighed, feeling all kinds of turmoil and dread, and opened the next letter.

Dearest Milton James,

I want to share this with you, these words I can't seem to find how to say, today of all days.

What we did last night was magical. Heaven was in my bed, in your arms, in your eyes. What you did to me . . . made me yours forever.

I had you inside my body, my dearest Milton James. I wish you were still there now.

You told me you loved me, and I told you the same.

But time always wins in the end. You left my bed before dawn, on this your last day here.

I joined your parents on the platform, not wanting to say goodbye. You, beautiful you, your train, your suitcase, your ticket in your inside coat pocket. You waved your farewell as the train pulled away, taking my heart with you.

I can still taste your goodbye kiss on my lips.

The gift you gave me last night fresh in my mind.

What we shared I will hold forever close. The way you held me, the way you touched me, the warmth of your hands on my skin. The way you moved inside me.

Nothing has ever felt so right.

I love you, Milton James. Now and forever.

I looked up from the letter, tears threatening to spill, and whacked Julian on the arm. "He left him! He actually went to freaking war. You said—"

"I said he didn't die," he replied, smiling sadly. He plucked a tissue from the box and handed it to me. "Read the next letter."

The next letter? I was still trying to process *this* letter. "They had sex." I held up the letter like it was proof. "They made love and he left him. My heart can't take this kind of thing. I'd prefer to watch insurance ads on TV with puppies and cry over that. Actually, I'd prefer to watch *Silence of the*

Lambs with the freaky human skin suit or a horror movie with mannequin body parts."

I shuddered violently at the thought and Julian put his hand over mine and gave it a squeeze.

"Read the next one."

I tried to hate his gorgeous smiling face, but I just couldn't.

I took the next letter out while Julian re-read the one I'd just handed him. I grumbled as I opened it but reluctantly, I began to read.

Dearest Milton James,

It's been four days, four long and awful days since you left. I didn't know a human heart could feel like this. How does it continue to beat when it's so broken? How does everyone keep living when it all feels so lost to me?

I'm trying to keep my chin up like you said. To make my own life like you said.

I applied for university, against my father's better judgement. He wanted me to stay but this town is not for me. First semester starts in February, and I'll be moving to Sydney then. I'm trying to save as much money as I can before I go, and I took the temporary job at the council.

I didn't know what else I could do. It all seems kind of pointless to me, but I think of how brave you are and it gives me the strength to plan ahead.

I think of you every waking moment, of what we did. I can still feel your touch, and when I'm alone in my bed at night, I relive every detail.

Every day I get through without you is a day closer to seeing you again.

All my love,

Raymond

I looked up at Julian, stunned. "We have a first name."

He smiled. "We do."

And then because I'm me, I began to cry. "We have a first name." Julian handed me a clean tissue and I dabbed at my eyes. And then I realised what letter was next. "There's only one more letter."

Julian nodded and carefully took it out of the envelope and handed it to me. I was too excited to ask him any questions. It was addressed as they all were.

Dearest Milton James,

I spoke to your mum in the street and asked her, probably far too excitedly, for any news. It's been over a week since you've been gone and I miss you so damn much, words can simply not convey.

She said you were at Duntroon and were keeping well, that you'd been assigned an administration role.

I asked what that meant.

She said you'd be an accounting clerk. Too good with numbers for boots in the mud, the accountant general had said. It wasn't likely you'd be deployed at all, your mum explained. Stationed in Duntroon for now. She was still proud and ever so relieved her boy wouldn't be sent off to war.

I almost cried in the street. I almost wept in front of your mother.

And I knew then, as if a light shined through the clouds, it didn't matter if you didn't write like you said you would. You would be safe and that was all that mattered.

I love you, Milton James. And I somehow love you more in your absence. I will wait for as long as it takes.

Yours, always.

I read the last part again and closed the letter with a sigh. "Is that it?"

"That's the last letter, yes."

I turned the letter over, as if there would be some magic ink on the back. Of course there wasn't. "It just feels . . . unfinished."

"Because it is," Julian said quietly. "We don't know what happened."

"It's like reading a book with the final chapter ripped out. This is like my worst nightmare."

"I thought fake body parts and human skin suits were your worst nightmare."

"They are. And books that don't end makes three."

He smiled at me, soft and lovely. "Hopefully we can find out what happened."

"I'll need to add to my notes," I said quietly. "I'm kinda bummed now. There's no closure. I hate that."

"But it reads as though he didn't go to war. He was stationed here in Australia, and Raymond, the man who wrote the letter, said he'd wait."

"Do you think they saw each other again?"

Please say yes. Please say yes.

"I'd like to think so, yeah." Julian rubbed my arm. "Maybe Raymond went off to uni in Sydney like he said he was going to and Milton, or whatever his real name is, took his leave in Sydney so they could be together away from their small, nosey town."

"Sounds nice." And totally unbelievable, but I didn't say that. I settled on a sigh instead. "I wanted . . . an ending. I wanted them to be happy."

"We don't know what the ending will be like. If we can even find them." Julian studied my face for a moment. "Do you still want to try and find them?"

"Yes. Now more than ever. I need to know what happened."

He smiled, the kind of smile that creased the corners of his eyes. Christ, he was handsome.

"Well, we can start looking tomorrow. Now we're all read up, we can begin searching."

I nodded. "In between running cages of parcels, boxes, and letters."

"Yes, and on that note, I should go home."

He looked like he didn't want to leave. I didn't want him to leave, but we'd decided that probably wasn't a good idea.

Hadn't we?

"Uh, yeah, sure," I said. "Probably."

He packed up the letters and I walked him to the door and opened it, though neither of us took another step. It was awkward and exciting; my heart was thumping, and my belly was all swoopy.

"Thank you for dinner," he said. "I really enjoyed spending the evening with you."

Was he being formal because he was nervous? I wasn't really sure what a gentleman would say, given most guys I'd had back to my flat usually left without so much as a goodbye.

"I really enjoyed you being here," I replied.

"I meant what I said. If we shouldn't date, like we talked about, then maybe you might want to hang out or grab dinner sometime . . . We don't have to talk about it at work if you'd rather no one else know."

"I'd like that," I said, my blood buzzing. I wasn't sure what the protocol was for this kind of evening and figured a polite goodbye kiss couldn't hurt. I leaned up on my toes and softly kissed his cheek. "Thank you."

Julian smiled and took a few steps out the door into the hall, but then he stopped and turned. His cheeks were pink, his bottom lip was between his teeth, but he was still smiling. "You know," he said, his voice pure sex. "I'd really like to kiss you properly, just once."

Holy fuck.

I grinned, almost laughed, and had barely nodded once before he strode back to me, pushed me against the door frame, and kissed me.

And when I say he kissed me, I mean *kissed*.

He pinned me with his body against the door jamb, one hand held my jaw, his other hand went to my lower back. His mouth, his tongue, his passion, the grunt he made.

My knees gave out but he held me there, pressed hard in all the right places. I wanted to wrap my legs around him, I wanted him to do every good and terrible thing to me he could imagine . . .

But then he pulled his mouth from mine. He pressed his forehead to mine for a second while we caught our breath. He wore a wicked grin with swollen lips and lust in his eyes. He thumbed my bottom lip and when I thought my heart was going to actually explode, he took a step back and let me find my feet.

He grinned and nodded. "Thought so."

He thought so what?

I couldn't think. I could barely stand. And he walked down the stairs, smug as fuck. "See you tomorrow, Malachi."

I was so dazed, I must have stood there for five minutes trying to get my scrambled brain back online and my lungs to take in oxygen. I managed to get inside where I promptly slid to the floor against the door, grinning like a fool, my head still spinning.

I took out my phone and called my emergency contact. She picked up on the second ring. "Better be important, bitch. I'm watching episode forty-three—"

"He kissed me," I blurted out. "Julian kissed me. And when I say kissed, I mean the man knows *how* to fucking kiss. Moni, he . . . fucking hell. Can he kiss."

There was a beat of silence. Then a shriek. "What the fuck, Malachi? Tell me everything."

CHAPTER TEN

JULIAN PUSHED me down on the bed, pressing his weight onto me. He lifted my leg and hitched it around his hip, our erections gliding against each other, slick with precome.

The friction, the heat, the building pressure was delicious.

His kiss was demanding and consuming. His firm hands left no doubt as to what he wanted, clawing at my skin, desperate and delicious.

Then he slicked himself with lube and was just about to push inside me. I wanted it so bad. I stroked myself, and I edged closer with each pass, ready for him to be in me, to fill me. I'd never wanted anything more. I was so close, so ready to come, so . . .

A beeping sounded, out of time with my hand on my cock, out of time with our rhythm.

More beeping and Julian disappeared. His kiss, his weight, his heat . . . gone.

My hand stilled and my alarm continued to fucking beep.

Fuck.

A dream.

I hated dreaming.

Fucking hated it.

I tried to close my eyes and get dream-Julian back. I tried to picture him, to feel him. He was just about to fuck me, goddammit. I tried giving my dick a few long strokes. I tried to recapture the moment . . .

And then my phone beeped again because I must have hit Snooze instead of Stop.

I considered throwing my phone but realised then it would just be beeping at me from across the room, so I hit the screen repeatedly until the noise stopped.

My dick had lost all interest, and now I was pissed off.

Fucking hell.

I was still mad in the shower, I was still mad when I got dressed, and I was still mad on the bus to work. I was still mad when I got there.

"Oh wow," Paul said when I walked in. "I read somewhere that NASA was missing reflectors from the Hubble. Didn't realise they made them into wearable pieces."

I looked down at my jacket. It was reflective silver. It matched the patches on my boots. Not that Paul could appreciate that. I met his serial-killer beady eyes. "I wore this so you could have a real long, hard look at yourself."

Cherry smiled, Theo laughed, and even Paul conceded a nod. "Good one."

After I smiled for Theo and sniffed my disdain in Paul's general direction, I sat down beside Cherry. "Morning," she said with her usual lack of enthusiasm.

I sipped my coffee. "Hm."

She ignored my petulance. "The boss isn't wearing brown again. Navy and white today. Looks all right too."

I kept my coffee mug at my lips, trying hard to remember the way he kissed me last night. "Hm."

Her gaze shot to mine and she leaned forward. "You're blushing."

"No I'm not." I lifted my cup higher to try and hide my face. "I'm absolutely not."

"Holy shit. What happened?"

"Nothing!" I peeked at her from around my cup and her eyes were as wide as her smile.

"Holy shit. And that was the worst attempt at lying I've ever seen."

I put my coffee on the table and took out my phone. "Siri, how can I be a better liar?"

"What happened between you two?"

And then, of course, Julian walked in. Mine and Cherry's conversation stopped right there and my face burst into flames. Not literally, obviously. But it sure felt like it.

"Morning," he said, ever so casual. He was wearing navy pants, different to yesterday's. I could tell by the stitching, and these shaped his arse a whole lot nicer. And a white button-down shirt with the sleeve cuffs rolled once.

Just once.

Like it was a whole other level of sexy.

"Morning," everyone else said.

I was still staring at his forearms.

"Morning," I said belatedly. I also sounded like an eighty-year-old woman who smoked two packs of cigarettes a day, which earned me a strange look from Cherry, which of course I ignored.

Julian turned around to face us, his fresh-made coffee in both hands. He sipped it, smiling when Denise walked in. "Another big caseload today. Cages galore down the back. And boss, your phone's ringing."

Julian ducked out of the breakroom, but 'cages galore' meant we were in for a busy day, but without too much grumbling, everyone washed their coffee cups and began their day. Cherry waited until we were alone. She washed her cup and I waited my turn. "So you and Julian, huh?"

"No," I replied. She shot me a disbelieving look and I could feel my face was on fire, so I gave up trying to lie. "We decided that it would probably be a bad idea."

"Oh." Cherry frowned and began drying her cup. "Why?"

"Just complicates things, you know? I like my job and he likes his job . . ." I began washing my cup. "If things get messy, it gets complicated."

"And your dad is his boss."

I cringed. "Yeah well, I'm just going to pretend that's not a thing."

She almost smiled. "It only gets complicated if you let it."

Julian walked in then and came straight over to the kitchenette. I moved from washing my cup to drying it. Cherry backed out of the room quicker than goth lightning, smiling as she went.

Then it was just me and Julian.

I didn't want things to be awkward between us, so of course, I made it super awkward. "I'm still mad at you, just so you know."

Julian paused, then turned to me. "About last night? You didn't seem too mad when I left."

I scowled at him. "No, not that. Not the kiss," I whispered. "Christ, you can do that to me any time you want. Right here if you're game."

He smiled but was obviously confused. "Then why are you mad at me?"

"Because I was having a dream about you. A very nice dream, if you get my drift. And just when it was getting to the really good part, my alarm went off and you disappeared."

His brow knitted and he gave a nod. "Right. So dream-me, not real-me, is in trouble."

"Correct. Well, both, but mostly dream-you."

"How can I be in trouble for something I didn't do?"

"But you did do it."

"In your head."

"Yes."

Julian chuckled and nodded slowly. "Right. Soooo, you dreamed of me?"

"Well, yes. But I—"

"And it was a nice dream, you said. And we were getting to the really good part . . ."

"Yes." My heart was squeezing a little too tight, my belly full of butterflies. "But I can't be held responsible. The way you said goodnight was hardly fair."

He smirked and made a low grunting sound of approval that lit me up inside. His eyes went to my lips. "So what was I doing to you in this dream?"

Holy fuck.

He was playing me like a violin.

I needed to resume some control or I was going to climb him like a freaking tree. "You were washing the dishes and vacuuming the floors. It made me really happy because I hate housework. You were just about to clean the bathroom when I woke up."

His eyes met mine and he smiled. "You're a terrible liar."

"So I keep getting told."

"Oh well. Maybe I'll finish the bathroom when you dream of me again tonight."

"You're awfully confident."

"You're awfully cute."

He was so close now. Was he standing this close a second ago? I wasn't sure. He smelled good too.

"I didn't think we were doing this at work," I mumbled, dazed by his stupidly attractive face. "Actually, I didn't think we were doing this at all."

He studied my eyes, searching for what I didn't know. "We probably shouldn't. You're right."

"And you probably shouldn't have kissed me last night," I breathed.

He was definitely standing closer.

"I probably shouldn't have. Yet I can't bring myself to regret it."

"Me either."

He lifted his hand as if to touch my cheek but then remembered where he was. He snapped out of whatever trance we were in, breaking our connection, and took a step back. "I thought saying no . . . to doing your housework was a good idea, but now I don't know."

I snorted. "My housework."

He chuckled. "I would very much like to do your dishes and vacuuming."

"Pretty sure I wouldn't object to just getting straight down to cleaning the bathroom," I said with a shrug. "If you know what I mean."

He grinned and looked back to the door before fidgeting with his fingers. "Being with you is fun. I forgot what fun was like. But if it's okay with you, maybe we could start with the dishes, then progress to some vacuuming. Cleaning the bathroom would be great, don't get me wrong.

But dishes and vacuuming are important too, don't you think?"

At this point, I really wasn't sure. "Just so we're clear, we're talking about things like dinner and conversation and some making out and more kissing like you kissed me last night because, holy fuck, yes please. And cleaning the bathroom is mind-blowing sex, right? Because in my dream, that's what it was and this conversation is completely metaphorical and I just want to be sure what I'm actually agreeing to. I mean, if you want to come to my place and actually clean my bathroom, I won't stop you."

Julian laughed. "Yes, metaphorically, we're on the same page."

"Oh good."

"So maybe we should do the basic housework first, like dishes and vacuuming. I'm all for that. I think we could then establish if we're prepared to move onto bathroom cleaning before it gets any more complicated. Given we work together and need to have . . . professional boundaries."

"Like this conversation?"

He laughed again. "Discussing housework is acceptable."

This whole conversation was unbelievable. "I'm glad."

"So . . ."

"Dishes at my place need doing again," I suggested. "Plus, I added more to the notes for the Milton James letters and I did a quick google but couldn't find anything. I didn't get very far. My brain was a little scrambled last night when you left. I had to vacuum and clean my own bathroom a few times, if you get what I mean."

Julian laughed, a warm, rumbling sound. "Should I apologise for that?"

"Oh, believe me, no apology necessary. Unless you want to apologise for disappearing in my dream just when the bathroom really needed a good clean."

He grinned and looked at the door again. We really had been in here too long. "So, tonight . . . ?"

I nodded. "Sure." Then I remembered something. "Can I ask you what you meant last night? When you were leaving, you said something like, 'Yeah, that's what I thought.'"

For the first time, he looked a little embarrassed. But his eyes met mine and he pierced me with his gaze. "I wondered how you'd respond. How you'd taste."

Oh, holy fucking fuck.

My knees felt wobbly.

"And?"

"And it was as good as I thought it would be."

My left knee buckled, and my head spun. "I think I need to sit down."

He chuckled again. "So, tonight . . ."

All I could do was nod, and he left the room with a smirk.

Arsehole.

I put my hand to my forehead and took a deep breath. The only reason I didn't have a hard-on right now was because my brain had short-circuited from the rest of my body.

404 Error. Erection Not Found.

Being able to walk and talk wasn't looking too good either. Until Cherry poked her head around the door. She wore a curious smile. "Everything okay?"

I nodded and shook my head at the same time, my hand still on my forehead, and my breathing was kinda weird. "Sure," I squeaked.

She laughed. "Good. You're already behind on your first cage."

Oh right. Work. I had to actually tell my legs to move, one in front of the other, to meet her at the door. "Sorry. Brain's a little scrambled."

She grinned, and as we walked together down aisle D, she said, "You're telling me everything at lunchtime."

"YOU AND CHERRY looked like you were having a cosy chat at lunch?"

Julian and I were in his car on the way to my place after work. It was drizzling rain, kinda miserable, and he was coming to my place to . . . do the dishes and maybe some vacuuming. Which, if you haven't caught up yet, was code for dinner and making out.

He was driving, of course, and his question threw me a bit. He was smiling but there was an edge to it, and I knew I had to come clean.

"I told her you kissed me," I blurted out. "I'm sorry but she asked why I was all flustered and had lost my ability to speak or think, and you know I can't lie. It's been well established. So I told her that we were working on the Milton James letters—which yes, I also told her about. I warned you that I cannot keep a secret, sorry about that—and she said, 'Oh my god, what is going on between you two? The pheromones are suffocating,' and then with the letters and you being at my place last night, and how you kissed me so fucking good my ancestors thanked you—"

He blinked.

"I'm sorry, but it all just came out and you know I can't stop talking when I get nervous but she promised not to tell anyone. And she will keep her word. She can keep secrets. I, on the other hand, cannot. I'm sorry."

Julian concentrated on traffic for a second before he smiled. "Your ancestors thanked me?"

"Right back to the Middle Ages."

He laughed and shook his head.

"You're not mad at me?" I asked. "I'm sorry. She asked and I panicked."

"I'm not mad. I'd rather anyone else at the office didn't know, but I can't be mad at you for telling the truth." He sighed. "I like that you can't lie."

"Technically, I *can* lie. I just look like I'm being Tasered while trying."

"Tasered?"

"Yes. High voltage impairment of physical function. A glitch in my matrix, an error 502 Bad Gateway kind of response." He laughed and I pouted. "I also had the same reaction when you kissed me last night and when you did all that dirty talk today about doing the dishes and vacuuming and cleaning the bathroom. That was when Cherry knew something was up because I was still malfunctioning when she found me."

Julian laughed and shot me a warm smile. "I just never know where a sentence is going to go when we talk."

I rolled my eyes. "Yeah, it's all cute now. Just wait a year when you'd rather stab yourself in the ear with an ice pick than have a conversation with me."

Julian raised an eyebrow. "A year, huh?"

God.

"I'm not implying that we'll still be . . . doing dishes or cleaning each other's bathrooms in a year. I was, more to the point, implying you'll want to stab yourself in the ear rather than listen to me prattle on. Well, god, I made this awkward. I'm sorry. I wasn't implying anything. No need to panic. I'm not drawing any conclusions about where this is going or even how it's going to work out. There's no pressure. I'm not a pressure kind of guy. It's just a 'let's do the dishes and see how things go' deal, right? God, I'm trying so hard to shut up right now—"

Julian held his hand out to me, palm up, across the centre console of his car. What was I supposed to do with it? Hold it?

Oh.

I slid my palm into his, he laced our fingers, and he placed our joined hands on my knee. I stopped talking. In fact, we never spoke another word all the way back to my house.

We just held hands.

CHAPTER ELEVEN

"SO, what I have so far is . . ."

Julian and I were on my couch, there were takeaway containers on the coffee table with glasses of mineral water, and Buster Jones was asleep on the lino floor after I'd given him a chicken snack.

Julian and I had managed not to maul each other's clothes off the second we walked through the door. Mostly thanks to Buster Jones who was meowing rather rudely at my balcony door. Julian had ordered dinner this time and it was delivered in no time at all.

I wondered if Julian would pounce on me the second we got inside, but he obviously decided that a long, smouldering eye-fuck would be more effective.

He wasn't wrong.

I couldn't stop looking at his eyes.

"Yes? What you have so far is . . .?"

Oh right.

I looked at the notes I was holding. "Notes. On the letters. The Milton James letters." My brain was a steaming pile of goo. "You have to stop looking at me like that."

"Like how?"

"Like you want to skip cleaning the dishes and vacuuming and move straight on to cleaning the bathroom."

He laughed, carefree and lovely. That deep voice of his did swoop and shiver things to my insides. "Well, you're cute. I can't help it."

"I'm cute?"

"Yes. You told me, to my face, that I was attractive. Why can't I say the same about you?"

"Because I have very little control over what comes out of my mouth, and that's not an excuse you can use."

He smiled but there was a serious edge to it. "I'm not using any excuse. You are cute."

"Cute in a good fun way, or cute in a childish, patronising way?"

"Definitely good and fun." He shrugged. "I wasn't joking when I said you were like sunshine and that I'd forgotten what fun was. Hanging out with you is different and exciting, definitely not what I'm used to."

"What are you used to? What kind of guys?"

"The boring, sensible ones. And I guess that suited me. I'm not the outdoorsy type or the adventurous type, really. My ex and I would have dinner parties and all that pretentious bullshit. When what I wanted to be doing was having themed movie nights, like 80s or sci-fi, cuddled up on the couch. Or going to art shows. Or to make food passports and eat all the different nationalities cuisines we've never eaten before. What he wanted to do was pretend he wasn't turning thirty and do lines of coke with random men in nightclub bathrooms."

Oh man.

"What was his name? Your ex. I need to know what name to curse every time I hear it."

"Christopher."

"Not Chris?"

"Oh no, Christo*pher*."

"Well, I hope he's decidedly miserable and I hope karma craps on him from a very great height."

Julian smiled. "I don't really care what karma does to him anymore."

"What kind of tosser wouldn't think that a food passport is *the* best thing ever? You could make a little booklet and have stamps for every meal from around the world you eat. I love that idea."

"I know, right? It sounds fun."

"And if there wasn't a restaurant or café, we could buy the ingredients and just make it instead. I don't know what the odds are of finding an authentic Andorran or Kyrgyzstan cuisine here in Sydney, so we might have to google it and make it ourselves."

"You just said we."

I tried to play it off and be cool about it. "Well yes, if we decide that we're not well suited for . . . vacuuming and cleaning each other's bathrooms, then there's no reason we can't still hang out and try all 195 cuisines from around the world."

"I'd like that."

"Same." Then I added, "But just so we're clear, I'd really like the housework thing to be a thing, but I'll understand if it's just not going to work out. At any rate, I'm glad we can talk about it."

"I am too. And yeah, just so you know, I appreciate your honesty and candour."

"Being open and upfront is the only way to avoid the bullshit, yes? Especially given we work together."

"Very true."

"And speaking of honesty and being upfront, did you want me to go through this list of notes on the Milton James letters, or should we just forgo the formalities and start making out?"

He chuckled and it ended with a moan. "I can't believe I'm going to say this . . . but the letters? If we're going to take our time and be responsible . . ."

"Oh my, your self-control is made of steel!"

"Made of stupidity," he mumbled. "I can't believe I'm going with the letters over the opportunity to kiss you again."

"I never said you couldn't kiss me after we read the notes."

He rolled his eyes. "Then hurry up and read them to me."

I very briefly entertained the idea of chucking the notes over my shoulder and climbing on top of him, straddling him, and kissing him for all he was worth. But we were being adults, apparently . . .

I took a deep breath and read my notes out loud. "You probably know all this already, considering you did try and find our Milton James."

"I didn't try very hard. I googled about three things and decided not to pursue it."

I nodded, because that was fair enough. "Okay, so they lived in a small town that had no cinema. They needed to go to the next town for the movies, so we can assume their town was a satellite town to a larger town. No more than an hour away, I would think. There was a road outside the town called Acacia Road that led to the creek slash river where they swam. That should be a pretty good lead if we can narrow it down further. And I'm assuming this all took place in the centre band of New South Wales, because when they talk of going to the city, they say Sydney. If it's the southern part of the state, they might go to Melbourne, or up north, they'd probably go to Brisbane because they're geographically closer. Their town had a council office. Well, their town had a council office back in the early 70s. There was a hardware store owned by a Mr Killian that had an alley behind it. Maybe we could access business registration details for that time and see if we can find a Mr Killian. That would at least give us a town."

Julian smiled. "Good idea."

"What did you find when you searched?"

"There was an American guy named Milton James who acted and did a lot of voice-over work in video games. But he didn't start a public life until a decade after these letters were written. Most internet searches lead to him. There was a real estate office and a lot of notices from the war memorial for servicemen from the world wars. So I refined the search for earlier decades, given Milton is an older generational name. I thought if this was written in the 70s and they're referring to someone who was already quite older, I should start looking as far back as the 1920s." He shrugged. "But we know Milton James isn't his name. Raymond says one day he'll call Milton by his real name. And one thing that hasn't changed over the decades is that teenagers idolise famous people, right? So I looked at actors and singers because most teens are into that. There was no internet back then, so they had to be famous by some popular media means. Maybe. Who would know."

"It could be a painter," I suggested. "Or a famous English poet from the 1700s they learned about in school. Oh, hang on, that was John Milton."

"Exactly." Julian nodded slowly. "It could be any famous James or Milton."

"Or it could be completely fictional. Or maybe one of them lived on Milton Street, or it was his middle name. Or maybe he just liked how it sounded."

"There are quite a few James Miltons as well. Both names are interchangeable for first or last names." Julian sighed. "I think looking for outside clues is our best bet, like you said. The hardware store owner or the name of the road. Then maybe we'll find something that makes it all link together. There's also the town named Milton which doesn't help in searching."

I nodded and pulled over my laptop and put Google to work.

I came up with exactly nothing on the name front. Well, lots of hits, but like Julian said, it went nowhere. We needed to get a town first.

I typed in *Killian Hardware rural NSW* for a broad sweep, not expecting any results and got exactly that. So then I went to the National Archive website and Australian Company Records, tried a few different variations and dates, but came up with exactly nothing.

When I looked up at Julian, I found Buster Jones was now on his lap purring and Julian was smiling at me.

I'd never wanted to be a cat so much in my life. "Excuse me, that's not fair," I said, offended. "Why is he allowed on your lap and I'm not?"

Julian laughed. "Technically, I never said you weren't allowed."

I gasped and gestured to my laptop. "You said I had to do this first." Then I squinted at him. "Actually, you said you wanted to do all kinds of housework, then you said we shouldn't do any kind of housework, then you said we could, then we kind of said we shouldn't, and now I'm allowed on your lap. And all this back and forth, I'm so confused, I don't know if we are or if we're not—"

Julian put poor Buster Jones on the floor and took my laptop and slid it onto the coffee table before taking my hands and looking me dead in the eye. "I want to see you, Malachi. I want to spend time with you. I know work complicates that and I'm sorry. I tried to not want you and I tried to ignore how I feel, but here I am. I want to be more than friends with you. The more time I spend with you, the more I like being with you. And if you want to climb onto my lap like the cat, I certainly won't stop you."

Oh wow. My heart felt like it was about to escape out of my chest. I couldn't remember how to breathe.

Then he ran his hand through his hair. "But . . ."

Ugh. There was always a but.

"But what?"

"But I'm your boss."

"I know."

"So I know we talked about this before, but I need you to know that nothing at work changes. You'll still act like a good employee and I'll still be a fair boss. I don't expect any more or any less from you. And you don't expect any more or any less from me. There's no pressure. If you decide you don't want to see me, you have my word, Malachi, that your job is protected."

"Thank you."

"I don't want anyone to think I coerced you or made you think you needed to be with me to keep your job."

I snorted. "Anyone who knows me knows I can't be coerced into doing anything I don't want."

He smirked. "You didn't want this job when you first started."

"No, I didn't think I'd stay. I wasn't opposed to starting. I was opposed to staying."

He laughed at that. "And now you want to stay."

"I do. The people I work with are great, and the boss is really fucking sexy."

"Is that right?"

I nodded slowly. "And as luck would have it, he's on my couch right now. And he has a look in his eyes that's setting my insides on fire."

His smile turned into something sultry and delicious. "I'd really like to kiss you right now," he whispered, low and rough.

"I'd really like you to kiss me right now." I don't even know how I managed to speak, let alone take his glasses off. Those umber-coloured eyes burned into me.

He slid his hand along my jaw and swiped his thumb across my bottom lip, ever so gently. His eyes never left mine, dark and intense, as he pulled me in for a kiss.

His lips were soft and warm, and it was sweet and chaste . . . until he tilted my head just so and opened my lips with his own. His other hand was on my neck, up my throat, and in my hair, and his tongue was in my mouth. He was owning this kiss, and he was owning me along with it.

I was putty in his hands, to be shaped and plied as he saw fit.

The way he kissed me last night had been amazing, but this was different. There was tenderness in this kiss, along with the man-handling and apparent daddy vibes I didn't know I needed.

There was no doubt about it. He was one hundred per cent in charge and I fucking loved it.

He kissed me deep, he kissed me sweet, he cradled my

face, my jaw, ran his fingers through my hair. It was sensory overload, but it wasn't enough.

I needed to feel him against me, in all the right places. But being side by side on the couch wasn't ideal. I broke the kiss, either so my soul could leave my body or so I could breathe. I wasn't sure at this point. And I pushed up and swung my leg over his thighs so I could straddle him.

He looked up at me, surprised but smiling, and this time I cupped his face in my hands and kissed him. His hands went to my hips and around my back and he pulled me in closer and . . .

Holy fuck.

The sound he made, the groan, the pained, guttural moan that rumbled from somewhere inside him shot sparks along every fibre of my body.

I tried to grind on him, to rub and push. I wanted to feel him, but his hands on my hips held me still. "Malachi," he murmured against my mouth. It was a plea, a warning.

I whined, of course, like a kid who couldn't have ice cream because he didn't eat his veggies.

"We should cool it a bit," he said with a wince. "It's been a long time for me and my body's not used to it."

"Oh. Sorry. Need me to help with something?"

He laughed and ducked his face into my neck. His warm breath and wet lips were sublime. "No, I'll be fine."

Except, his lips on my skin sent a shiver through me. He grunted and I laughed. "That was your fault." But I'd heard what he'd said, so I pulled back a little to sit more on his knees rather than grind against his crotch. I thumbed his cheek, his jaw, I pecked his pink, swollen lips. His eyes couldn't seem to focus. "Can you see me without your glasses?"

He smiled. "Yes. You're the most beautiful blur I've ever seen."

I laughed and kissed him again, and again, and again, teasing his lips with the tip of my tongue, just enough to make him growl at me.

"I'm trying to be good," he said, slowly closing his eyes. "You're not making it very easy."

"I'm sorry." I pulled away and he let me go, which was a little disappointing, not gonna lie. I gave him back his glasses and took his hand and kissed his palm. "But you're incredibly good at kissing. If I could leave a Yelp review, it'd be five stars, would totally recommend, will hopefully be doing it again soon."

He laughed and fixed his glasses, then took my hand again. "You have no idea how much I didn't want you to stop. But we're easing into doing the housework, right? Making sure it's what we both want before we just start on scrubbing the bathrooms."

I nodded reluctantly. "Yeah. I know. And I do appreciate that. But we can do some light housework, right? Dishes, clean some windows, a bit of dusting."

"I would very much like that. I just got a little overheated, sorry."

"Don't apologise. It's a compliment."

He sighed. "Are you done working on the letters for tonight?"

"I might try googling some more stuff later. Pretty sure I'll be watching some . . . housework hub when you leave."

He chuckled. "Housework hub."

"Yeah. Like GayHub but for . . . well actually it's just straight-up GayHub. Calling it housework hub felt weird. I was just trying to keep the joke going."

"Maybe next time we could progress to some other light

housework duties," he said, his cheeks pink. "I could take you out for dinner or to a tapas bar or something first, if you like."

"Like a proper date?"

He made a face. "Well, yes. But is me coming here for takeout not a date?"

Well, shit.

"I guess so. I wasn't sure what to call it, to be honest."

So that would make this our second date? I was too scared to ask.

He smiled shyly and played with my fingers for a bit. "Would Friday night suit you? For dinner?"

"Friday night sounds great. Can we do the food passport thing? I love that idea."

He beamed a smile at me. "We absolutely can. Then I should get going now and leave you to . . ."

"Watch porn."

He groaned. "You're not making it easy to leave."

I kissed him, my hand to his cheek, honestly just about to tell him to stay when my phone rang. Of course the word *Mum* flashed up on the screen, which was the equivalent of a bucket of cold water.

"Ugh."

"You should get that," Julian said.

"I should throw my phone out the window," I said, then answered the call while disentangling myself from Julian. "Hey, Mum."

"Hello, darling."

Of course Julian stood up and readjusted himself. A rather large bulge in his pants.

"Jesus Christ."

"What's wrong?" Mum asked.

"Oh nothing," I whispered. "Just watching something

on the TV. Hang on one sec. Mum, can I call you right back? Gimme two minutes."

I disconnected the call and gawped at the huge—and when I say huge, I mean huge—dick-shaped bulge in Julian's work pants. I mean, I knew I could feel something when I was straddling him, but seeing it? It turned my bones to jelly.

Julian laughed. "Are you okay?"

"I really am," I said, still ogling his crotch. "Can't say I'll be saying the same after Friday night. Your dick is huge."

Julian laughed again and *re*-readjusted himself. I could tell he was a little embarrassed but he cupped my face in his hands, kissed me, and said, "I will make it so good for you."

Then he picked up his jacket from the back of the chair, and with a smug smile, he left me standing speechless and dazed in the middle of my loungeroom. Pretty sure I heard his laughter echo up the stairwell.

Still stunned, I collected my wits enough to realise I was still holding my phone. I sent him a quick text message.

Pleased to announce that this Friday we will be forgoing all dishes and vacuuming and moving straight onto scrubbing bathrooms.

His reply was almost immediate.

Or we could do dishes, vacuum, AND the bathrooms.

I had to sit down before I could reply.

So much housecleaning.

No reply was forthcoming and I assumed he was now driving home, so I called my mum back. She only wanted a chat, to ask me how I was still enjoying my new job, to ask me if I was eating okay, that I should come around for dinner soon, and to ask how Moni was doing.

I tried to be interested, but all I could think about was

Julian, his massive schlong, and his promise to make it good for me on Friday.

Lord.

He was assuming I'd even live to Friday. My heart was thumping rather peculiarly and my head was spinning just thinking about it. Not to mention that my testicles were buzzing at a constant one on a TENS machine. It was very likely that I could drop dead of horny anticipation before Friday.

"Okay, Mum, thanks for calling," I said as there was a break in her droning on. "I should go. I'll talk to you soon."

"Okay, love."

"Bye."

I ended the call and pulled my laptop over, trying to decide on what kind of porn I wanted when my phone rang again.

I groaned but saw it was Julian calling. "Hello?" I answered.

"I'm curious," he began, no small talk. "When you said 'so much housecleaning,' was my suggestion of dishes, vacuuming, *and* bathroom cleaning too much? Or are—"

"Okay, so I'm just going to stop you right there. One, there is no such thing as too much. And two, I had to listen to my mother talk nonstop for ten minutes and I only got off the phone with her right this minute so I've just opened GayHub and I'm trying to decide if I want to watch *Twink Gets Railed by Huge Cock* or *Daddy Makes His Boy Moan for Hours*. So does that sufficiently answer your question?"

His warm laughter sounded in my ear. "Okay, I was just checking. Wanted to be on the same page, that's all."

"Same page, same book, same library at this point. I'm going to go with the *Twink Gets Railed by Huge Cock* video.

Because I saw what you're packing so I better see what I'm in for. Research is very important."

He laughed again. "Then I'll let you get back to it. I'm just going to have a steaming hot, very soapy shower. I'll see you in the morning."

"You're a cruel man. Now I'm thinking I need to watch shower porn. Ugh. So many decisions."

"Good night, Malachi," he said, his voice low and soft. It sent a shiver through me.

"Good night, Julian."

I tossed my phone onto the couch beside me, grinning to myself. I decided on the twink-getting-railed porn and I wasn't disappointed. I needed a shower afterwards, which of course made me think of Julian in the shower and how, when he'd readjusted himself twice, he was basically moving his dick on his hip.

He was big.

Aaaaand then imagining it was me getting railed by him, I watched the *Daddy Makes His Boy Moan* video, and I needed to clean up again.

Before I fell asleep, I double-checked the calendar. Three days to go until Friday.

CHAPTER TWELVE

"WE HAVE a date on Friday night. Sex is definitely on the table. Some kind of sex, anyway. He has a monster cock. It's so big it could very well need its own postcode. And before you can ask, dear Moni, we talked about work and our responsibilities and all that boring adult stuff, and we decided that we could be worth the complication. He acknowledged his position of power, given he's my boss, and we talked about how that could affect us. But holy fuck, Moni, he kisses like the fucking devil. I'm telling you, my toes curl. He does this thing with his hands and his whole body when he kisses. It's not just his mouth. It's a whole-body experience and something I'm very much looking forward to experiencing a lot more of on Friday night. God, do you know how many times I had to jerk off last night after he left?"

"TMI, Malachi."

"You said to tell you everything."

"True. I did."

"Anyway, I'm just about to walk into work. I better get off the phone."

"You're taking me out for brunch on Sunday. Then we can hit up the second-hand store."

"Deal."

"And you can tell me everything that happened."

"There will be a lot of TMI."

"It's why I love you, Malachi."

"Awww."

"And Malachi?"

"Yes?"

"I'm happy for you."

"I'm happy for me too!" I almost did a little jig in the car park near the front doors to work. I was ridiculously happy.

This whole romance, getting to know someone, flirty-fun stage was a helluva ride.

I went inside and headed straight for the breakroom. I knew Julian was in his office—his car was in the car park—but I walked past. As a rule, I'd never stopped past his office first, so I wasn't about to start now. Regardless of how much I wanted to see him, how excited I was to see him, I made myself walk to the breakroom instead.

I spotted Cherry in her usual seat, her raven black hair covered her face with her head down as she read something on her phone. Paul and Theo were at their table, discussing something political that I was staying well-clear of, and I slid into my seat next to Cherry.

"Morning."

She looked up, her lipstick a dark dusty rose colour today instead of black. It matched a square of pink plaid on her otherwise black shirt, and it was amazing.

"Morning," she replied, expressionless as always.

"Love your lip colour."

"Thanks. Love your shirt."

I grinned. It was a lavender Care Bears shirt. The

chunk of purple in my hair was fading so I had to match it accordingly. My lavender Converse high tops were a perfect match. The black skinny jeans and distressed black jacket gave the whole fit enough credibility that I didn't look like an overgrown toddler.

"Can I ask a favour?" I asked. "I know you're super busy, but I believe your google-fu is the strongest in all the lands and I am yet to learn the ways."

She rolled her eyes and smiled, which I took as a yes. I took the folded piece of paper from my pocket. "Here are my notes. I was up early this morning trying to search online," I said. "But I didn't get far."

I handed them over, and while she read through it, I made myself a coffee. By the time I was done, she was nodding to herself.

"What do you think?" I asked.

"I've worked with less."

"So you'll help?"

"I'll try."

"Oh my god, thank you. I'll take some of your caseloads today to free up some time."

That earned me a smile. Then she eyed me cautiously. "Does Julian know I'll be helping?"

"I told him that I told you about me and him. I'm a firm believer in full disclosure." Then I shrugged. "And I lack the ability to keep secrets or to stop talking sometimes."

"Okay, I wasn't sure if I was hiding this." She nodded to the piece of paper. "Have you seen him today?"

"No, why?"

One perfectly sculptured black eyebrow raised slightly with a gentle tilt of her head. "He's back in brown. I wondered if you two had a fight or something."

"Oh, no, not at all. Actually, if anything it's the opposite . . ."

"Well, his pants are brown and his shirt is a cream-of-wheat colour but it's definitely tighter than he used to wear."

"Oh, that sounds like a school principal. That shouldn't be hot, right? Why does that sound so hot?"

She chuckled. "And there was also no tie, and his top two buttons were undone."

I gulped down my coffee. "Christ. I'll never make it to Friday."

There was a deafening beat of silence. "What's happening on Friday?"

"Nothing," I said far too quickly and probably a few decibels too loud and an octave too high.

Cherry stared, her dark gaze humoured and curious. "Mm-hmm."

And then, right on fucking cue, Julian walked in. His trousers were brown, yes. But they were well-fitted and bulged in all the right places. And his shirt . . . also fitted, sleeves rolled just once, top two buttons undone.

Fuck. Me.

Cherry nudged her foot to mine. "Close your mouth," she whispered.

I fumbled to put my coffee down before I spilled it all down my Share Bear shirt, and Julian smirked as he walked past me. "Morning," he said brightly.

He even had the audacity to smell good.

Jerk.

I leaned in toward Cherry. "Should we start on the list? At your desk?"

"Uh, sure," she agreed. She picked up the piece of paper. I took our coffees and made our way to the door.

"Oh, Julian," Paul asked. Theo was nodding beside him, smile wide. "What do you think of the state's government push for—"

Julian spun around to look at me, finding me at the door with an expression on his face that was a lot like 'help, I can't do politics with these two,' but I just gave him a wink before I made my escape. I put the two coffees on Cherry's desk and pulled my chair over to hers.

She chuckled. "Want to tell me what that was about and why you're grinning like Willy Wonka right now?"

"Oh, no reason."

"I take it things with you and Julian are going well?"

"He's a surprising amount of fun," I said, trying to play it cool. "And he's smart, and he's considerate, and—"

"And you like him."

My gaze shot to hers. "I do. It's crazy, and it's hellafast, but yes, I do." I leaned in and whispered behind my hand. "And when I say the man can kiss, I mean *kiss*. Like out-of-body-experience kind of kiss."

Cherry laughed. "Well, he seems happier. It's good to see him smile."

I couldn't help feeling happy about that, and a little proud if I was being honest. "Anyway," I said, patting the piece of paper with my notes on it. "I wrote down all I could find and what I narrowed my search down to, but I didn't have much luck."

I had it shortlisted down to twelve possible towns throughout the state, going from no cinema, one council office building, and the mention of classmates going to work in the mines. The road name out of town was more popular than I ever thought possible. Almost all towns had an Acacia Road, but even with all this, I'd hit a dead end.

"You actually refined it pretty well," she said. "But I

think I'll start with the hardware store owner because we have a name."

"I looked for half a second at the business registrations for that surname around the late 60s and early 70s but I didn't find anything."

She mumbled something about companies and proprietors but was already tapping away on her keyboard; then Denise came through on her way to the breakroom. "Cages are in," she said with her usual grin.

I was quick to my feet. "I'll start on yours," I said to Cherry before rushing to begin the first cage. It was only fair I help her with her quota when she was doing work for me.

I was almost halfway through the first cage before I saw Paul. "Everything okay?" he asked. "You've got a motor underneath ya today."

"Oh yeah, I'm fine," I replied, trying not to get caught up in conversation which would lead to questions—

"So what are you and Cherry working on?"

Questions exactly like that.

"Oh, it's nothing," I said, dropping my wrist like the queerest queer who ever queered.

"Hm." Paul's mouth was a thin line, matching the unimpressed crease of his brow. "Anyone ever told you that you can't lie for shit?"

"All the time, actually."

"So you are both working on something . . ."

"It's secret squirrel stuff. But it's approved. It's not like we're not doing work, because it is work-related. I just asked Cherry to help because she's good at the cryptic stuff."

He eyed me in that creepy serial-killer way. "Well, if you need any help . . ."

"I'll be sure to ask," I added cheerfully, because I was

sure this little chat had come to its natural end. "I better get back to work." I pushed the cart away, gave Paul a smile over my shoulder, and hightailed it out of there.

I got through my first cage, which was actually Cherry's, and started on mine, barely a few parcels in when Theo found me in the bottom of aisle L-M. "Oh, Julian was looking for you," he said, ever so casually.

"He was?"

"Yep."

"How long ago?"

He shrugged and gave me a goofy grin. "About five minutes."

"Better go see what that's about."

I wheeled my cart to the side wall and headed up to the front of the warehouse. Cherry had her head in some huge directory, her fingers trailing down the page. She looked engrossed and I didn't dare interrupt her, so I bypassed her and lightly tapped on Julian's office door.

"You wanted to see me?"

He looked up and grinned when he saw it was me. "Come in."

I stepped inside and closed the door behind me, quickly taking the seat opposite him. "Everything okay?"

"Yeah, of course. Why wouldn't it be?"

"I gave my notes on the Milton James letters to Cherry. I broke it all down and I tried to google stuff this morning at 6am because I couldn't sleep, but I kinda got to a dead end. I narrowed down the townships I think were possible. Anyway, I know we said we'd keep it on the down-low, but she's better at the Scooby-Doo stuff than me. Actually, she's more like Velma. I'm the Scooby-Doo one. Incredibly cute but not overly helpful."

Julian's smile widened. "Cherry would make a great Velma."

"You're not mad?"

"Not at all."

I sagged with relief. "Phew. Love that shirt, by the way. And the undone buttons at the top. Lord, I almost fell off my chair this morning."

"I noticed."

"You did it on purpose, didn't you? You deliberately decided against the tie, then undid one button, thought to yourself, 'Oooh, that's kinda hot. And you know what would be even hotter and what would make Malachi have visceral bodily reactions when he sees me? I'll just undo a second button. That oughta do it.'" I shook my head in mock disgust. "Cherry told me to stop drooling, by the way."

He chuckled, but his fingers went to his exposed neck and down to his collarbone, distracting me until he spoke. "That's exactly what I thought this morning."

"And the pants," I said with a sigh. "They fit very well, lemme tell you. Now I'll need to search up suit porn when I get home. So thanks for that."

Julian smiled at me for a long moment. "So I, uh, I have a meeting with your father this afternoon."

I stared at him, the blood draining from my entire head. I think I squeaked.

He laughed. "It's a monthly department head meeting. Nothing to panic about."

"Christ, Julian, you could have led with that." I pulled at the collar of my shirt. "Is it hot in here? Are the walls pulsing, or is it just me? I think the blood returned to my brain too fast." I tried to catch my breath. "Warn a guy next time."

He was still amused, apparently. "But I need to be in

the city by five and they usually run late. So I won't be able to drive you home today. I just wanted to let you know."

"That's fine. I don't expect you to."

"I know. I just . . . like doing that for you." He shifted in his seat. "I like . . ."

The way his voice dropped when he said that made my insides curl. "You like what?"

His gaze met mine. "I like . . . making sure you get home okay."

That was absolutely not what he meant. "I get the feeling you're not being absolutely truthful."

He laughed. "Driving you home gives me an excuse to see you."

"You don't need any excuse to see me. You just have to say you want to see me."

"I want to see you. Though that would be three night's this week, and we have plans for Friday night, which will make four, and I'm trying to decide if it's too much too soon."

"Eight o'clock at my place sound okay? Because the *Great British Bake Off* is on TV tonight, and if you want to bring some takeout to my place and we can get cosy on the couch, I will have absolutely zero objections."

Julian smiled all warm and lovely. "I can do that."

"And although I would like to stress that there is no pressure on you whatsoever for any housecleaning duties, I'd just like you to know that I'm very open to any possibilities. You know, like a little precursor for what you plan on doing to me this Friday night."

His nostrils flared, then he shook his head with a laugh. "I'm very open to any possible suggestions." He cleared his throat. "Though we probably shouldn't be talking about that here."

"No, we probably shouldn't." I stood up. "I have a lot of work to get done today, so I better get back to it." I walked to the door and stopped. "I'm thinking Japanese dumplings for dinner sounds great, and also when you're in the meeting with my dad this afternoon and he asks you how I'm going, which he probably will, look him right in the eye and try not to think about what you want to do to me tonight."

Julian's eyes lasered into me. "Now you're just being cruel."

"You can thank me later. And when I say thank, I mean punish." He glared at me and I gave him a sassy grin before I walked out. I only took two steps before Cherry spotted me.

"Oh, I think I found something."

"You did?" I zipped over to her. "Tell, tell, tell."

"Okay, so Mr Killian," she said, turning to the three huge directories open on her desk. Her computer had two minimised screens side by side. God, she should work for the Federal Police. "I found a Frankston Holdings company that registered, amongst others, a hardware store in 1953. Frankston Holdings' subsidiary director was a Mr George Killian."

"Mr Killian."

She nodded. "Business directories back then weren't as complete as they are now, but yes. George Killian's son, Peter Killian, was the lessee of Northbury Hardware from 1966 until 1985."

"Northbury. Where is that?"

Cherry opened a tab on her computer to reveal a Google Map. "Northbury. A town with a population of ten thousand, thirty kilometres west of Milldale, about five hours northwest of Sydney."

"Oh my god."

"Northbury in the early seventies had a population of approximately six thousand. Consisted of a primary school, a high school, a hardware store, convenience store, community swimming pool, and to this day it still doesn't have a cinema. Local council offices amalgamated with Milldale in the 90s, so there used to be council buildings but not anymore. Mining districts to the west and north. Northbury was founded by the Hindton River, and there's a road to the south of the town named after a family who settled there by the name of Acacia."

"Acacia Road." I couldn't believe it. "Holy shit. You found it. You found the town."

Cherry looked up at me from her seat. "Yep."

"Have you considered working for national security? Or like one of those catfishing shows? Because honestly, you should."

She smiled, a little proud. "But then I wouldn't be here to help you."

"This is very true. Cherry. You are an absolute champion."

She closed the first directory book with a thump. It was a huge black binder with pages of super flimsy paper with tiny writing. Then she stacked on the second one, having clearly done all she could do. "Now you can search up high school records for the years this Raymond attended and hopefully there was only one Raymond. It will make your job a lot easier. Facebook high school groups are unsurprisingly careless about the information they post. Or try the local newspaper. They have most of the records digitalised now, but some are still on microfiche."

"On what? What is a microfish?"

"Microfiche is old-school Google," Paul said behind me.

"If you need help using it for anything, I'm your man. Can find anything. Just need a little know-how."

Goddammit.

"Oh, thanks," I said. His offer was generous and I probably shouldn't exclude him so deliberately, but the fewer people knew about this the better. "I'll let you know."

"Is this the secret squirrel stuff?" he asked.

"Yes, it is."

"What secret squirrel stuff are we talking about?" Theo asked, suddenly appearing out of nowhere.

Nothing was secret in this place.

But Theo was always so bright and bubbly, it wasn't like I could be mad at him. "Oh, nothing. Cherry was just helping me with a case. She's very good at finding random clues."

"She sure is," he replied. "Anyway, it's morning teatime." And with the mention of that, Theo and Paul disappeared into the breakroom.

"I'm sorry," I said to Cherry. "I didn't mean to involve you in anything where you might have to lie to them. Here, let me carry these for you." I picked up the directories, which weighed a freaking tonne. *How had she carried them from . . .* "Where am I taking these?"

"This way," she said, taking the top binder. Down to the bottom storerooms near the back loading dock and where we collected the cages from, there were fire-safe cabinets that had all kinds of books and directories. One of the binders she'd been looking through was a business registry directory that looked older than Noah's ark.

"How do you even know where to start?" I asked.

She shrugged. "It might sound weird to you, but I love data collation. I love history records and censuses, that kind of thing." She locked the cupboards and gave me an awkward smile. "It's almost anthropological, in a way. Records of humans, names, and dates."

"Like on that show where they research celebrities heritage and find records of some distant relative in Ireland or Morocco that dates back three hundred years."

That earned me a smile. "Yeah. I guess. It's fascinating to me that a name in the census records was someone who lived, worked, married, or didn't. And the death notations, of course. Died of diphtheria at the age of thirty-four."

The mention of death details might have been odd, but I was talking to a goth girl.

"I've always wondered about people who lived in ancient times," I admitted as we began walking back toward the breakroom. "What kind of shoes they wore, how they made clothing from cotton by hand. Like how clever they must have been to know how to do that before anyone else. Without any machinery. And they dyed them using the most obscure powders and stuff. I wouldn't have lasted a day."

So yes, I realised, while she thought about human anthropological sciences, I thought about fashion.

No one should be surprised by this. Cherry certainly wasn't.

"It is fascinating," she said. "And once you learn how this data was recorded and kept, it makes it easy to find."

"Well, you deserve a gold star for your help today."

"It was no problem. It was fun. And you got through one whole cage for me already. We should swap more often."

I laughed. "Deal."

We grabbed a quick coffee but I needed to get back on the floor. I had my own cages to get done and I didn't even stop long for lunch. Just a quick bite and back at it, sorting letters and parcels, boxes of all kinds, padded envelopes, cards, bills, gifts. The incoming mail never seemed to end. But by five o'clock I was done. It had been super productive, I got lots done, and after a cheery wave to the gang as we all left for the day, I ran for the bus stop.

Not even the funky smell on the bus could dampen my spirits. I calculated by the time I got home and showered, washing off the warehouse dirt and grime. I'd have about two hours before Julian would turn up around eight.

That would give me two hours to see what the internet could divulge about a guy called Raymond who lived in Northbury in 1972.

CHAPTER THIRTEEN

NOTHING.

That's what I found on Raymond who lived in Northbury in 1972. I needed a surname, and I couldn't get that without accessing school records. And that was even if he went to high school in Northbury and not the bigger town half an hour away.

I searched Facebook, as Cherry suggested. Found plenty on Northbury and the high school, but only recent posts. I searched historical sites for that region of the state. I tried blanket variation searches of Raymond Northbury and, very unsurprisingly, found diddley squat.

His aunt Kath had worked at the council offices, so I searched Northbury Shire offices and found photos online of the buildings, but most news articles revolved around the amalgamation. I had no idea if Raymond's aunty married, so even if I could find the names of any women who worked there in 1972, which I could not, I wouldn't know what side of his family she was on or if her surname had changed when or if she married.

Another dead end.

So then I decided to switch gears. I couldn't find anything on Raymond so I decided to focus on his mystery man.

I typed in *Northbury Shire, Vietnam War*. Surely if some of the boys from the region were going to war, there'd be something in the local newspaper. The Milldale Star paper had proudly been in print since 1921, apparently. Or so the website said.

There were articles, yes. Mostly historical archive information, but . . . very little. Most just reported on the news, and any mentions of war were usually a small paragraph on page four or five.

For fuck's sake.

Then my phone rang and Julian's name appeared on-screen. I'd lost track of time and answered quickly. "Hey."

"Hello, I have a delivery of Japanese dumplings for a Mr Malachi Keogh."

I laughed and let him in. "Mmm, dinner and a snack."

He chuckled, and seeing my laptop and notes all over the couch, he put the takeout on my tiny dining table. "Been busy, I see."

"Yes. And I have much to tell."

His eyes went wide. "You found him?"

"No. I didn't. Cherry found the town using business registration information on the hardware store owner."

"But it wasn't in his name. I checked."

"No, it was some holdings company that owned a bunch of businesses, but there was a director and a son and a cousin three times removed and a billy goat guarding a bridge . . . She should work for homeland security. I'm not even kidding."

Julian smiled at me, then slid his palm along my jaw and pressed his lips to mine. It was warm and sweet and made me feel as light as a feather. "I've wanted to do that all day."

"Mmm," I hummed dreamily. "I would like you to do that to me all day."

"Dinner first? Sorry, I'm starving."

I laughed and grabbed two plates. "Yes, of course, and I can tell you what else I found. Or what I didn't find." Then I checked the time. "Holy shit, *Great British Bake Off* starts in ten minutes."

I relayed all of what I'd found and not found while we ate, then I shoved my laptop and papers onto the coffee table and propped a cushion at one end, patting it for Julian to sit lengthways on the couch. Which he did. Then I proceeded to plant myself between his legs, my head on his chest.

He wrapped his arm around my chest. "You good now? Comfortable?"

"Yep."

He chuckled and kissed the side of my head. It felt so good and so warm and comforting. I felt safe and . . . I felt his dick pressing against my lower back. And then, of course, my dick answered the call and I suddenly wasn't too interested in watching the TV.

I wiggled back a little bit and held his hand that was on my chest. His strong fingers threaded with mine, and he shifted to get more comfortable or to get more friction. I wasn't sure which.

Then, with the worst timing ever, I remembered . . . "Oh, how'd your meeting go with my dad?"

"It was fine," he murmured against my ear. His deep voice rumbled right through me. "I only spoke to him for about ten seconds. He asked how you were fitting in. I said you were the sexiest man I'd seen in a long time."

I laughed. "You did not."

His hand pressed down on my chest, his other hand gripped my hip, holding me against him. His dick was hard now. I might have groaned like a B-grade porn star. Julian's lips were at my ear, and his hand went from holding my hip to palming my cock. "I told him I had trouble controlling myself around you."

"Oh fuck."

"I said I wanted to hold out, to treat you right, but every time I see you, my body reacts." He kissed down my neck and rubbed my erection through my jeans. "Malachi, I've never wanted someone the way I want you."

His words, his breath in my ear, his hands set my insides on fire. I turned in his arms and claimed his mouth with my own. He pulled me flush against him, his hands sliding down to my arse, and he squeezed, grinding me against his huge cock.

Pleasure wrapped itself around my spine, sparking a fire inside me. Rubbing myself against him, feeling his arousal, his tongue in my mouth, his strong hands, his body underneath me.

Could I come like this?

I think I could come like this.

Just a bit more . . .

"Malachi," he breathed.

"More," I moaned. I sounded desperate, frantic. I *was* desperate and frantic.

God, this is so hot but not enough.

I needed more.

I pushed harder, I kissed him deeper, imagining his massive dick sliding into me just as he gripped my hips and thrusted, shuddering and groaning. His head pushed back, grunting from somewhere low in his chest, and he came.

His face was pure ecstasy; his eyes rolled closed, his neck corded, and he convulsed with a moan. But he held me tighter as he rode out his orgasm, bucking into me, and the feel of his cock pulsing between us was enough to send me over the edge.

He took a hold of my face and looked into my eyes as I came, watching with wonder and fire in his eyes. "Oh, Malachi," he breathed. "So beautiful."

When my mind returned to my body, my bones were made of jelly and all I could do was laugh, I collapsed on top of him, burying my face against his neck, breathing in the scent of him and the smell of our sex. We were a sticky mess but I couldn't bring myself to care.

"We missed the technical challenge," he said. "On the *Great British Bake Off.*"

I started to laugh. "I think we made our own. Ten out of ten. I'm still seeing stars."

Julian's hand found my hair. "We made a bit of a mess."

I reluctantly pulled myself up and unglued myself from him. "That means we can shower together."

He raised an eyebrow. "Is that so?"

I took his hand and pulled him to his feet. "Yep. And my shower is small, so we're gonna have to stand really close."

Still holding his hand, I led him to the bathroom, then peeled off my shirt and pulled my jeans down. I'd never been shy about being naked. I was a pale skinny guy with an average-sized dick, and I refused to feel shame for any part of me.

Julian, on the other hand, unbuttoned his shirt and let it fall from his shoulders. He wasn't as pale as me, but he was by no means tanned. He had a dusting of chest hair which I just had to run my fingers through. I don't remember ever seeing body hair on a guy I'd been with. Most of them shaved or waxed. But this . . .

"This is hot," I murmured. Then I tweaked his nipple, just because I could.

He unbuttoned his pants, unzipped, and pulled his briefs down over his thighs.

And I'm here to tell you . . . the man was hung.

You know in those porn movies when the skinny nerdy guy has a dick halfway down to his knees? Well, they exist in real life.

"Jesus fucking Christ," I breathed, staring at it. At him. "That is the biggest, most beautiful dick I've ever seen."

Julian's cheeks flamed pink. "It's . . . it's been an issue for some guys."

I put my hand to my chest. "Believe me when I say, I am not some guys. And my mum never raised no quitter."

Julian laughed and gave himself a slow pull. "I can ease you into it if you think you'd like to try."

"Now?" I asked. "I can be on my bed face down, arse up in two seconds."

He burst out laughing. "I thought we were waiting for Friday for the full cleaning of bathrooms."

"Well, I guess, if you want to . . ."

"Weren't we going to try a few other things first?"

"Like we did just now?"

"Tomorrow night you could come to my place. I'll make you dinner," he said, brushing his lips against mine. "I'd love to taste more of you."

My knees did that wobbly-jelly thing again. I let out a breathy laugh. "I'll have you know, I normally conduct myself with some modicum of decency, but you talk to me like that, and you touch me, and I turn into Insta-ho."

He laughed before kissing me with smiley lips. "Is that your superpower?"

"Uh, more like my kryptonite."

His cock, spent and hanging heavy, twitched between us and he kissed down my neck. "You are my kryptonite."

"Fucking hell," I breathed, giving him more of my throat.

He groaned and pulled back. "Maybe we should make this a cold shower."

Shower?

I looked around as if seeing we were in my bathroom for the first time. "Oh, right." I laughed and turned the water on. Julian followed me in and kissed me under the stream of water. He kissed me as we washed each other, and he kissed me when we dried off.

And he stood there in my tiny bathroom wearing nothing but a towel around his waist, with his wet hair and a goofy smile. And a semi-hard dick, which was mighty impressive given its length and girth.

But he never pushed me for more, which both impressed and disappointed me.

His trousers were mostly spared from his jizz, though his underwear and shirt went into the washing machine. My jeans, briefs and shirt were a splotchy mess, so I pulled on some old jogger pants and a T-shirt, then handed Julian a light knitted sweater.

It was fuchsia pink with a hot pink argyle pattern.

"Oh wow," he said, holding it up. "It's . . . a bold choice."

I snorted. "And it will look so hot on you."

"And tight."

"Exactly. That's why I chose it."

Julian laughed but pulled it over his head. I nodded because I was so right. "Tight, *and* hot."

He risked a glance at the mirror, then looked again. "That's actually not bad."

I put my hand to my chest and gave him an Oscar-winning imitation of Marilyn Monroe. "You may doubt my sincerity and doubt my good name, but darling, don't ever doubt my fashion sense."

Julian laughed and put his glasses back on. "Well, I think we missed the baking show."

"I'm okay with that."

"Me too."

"Sooo, tomorrow night. Did you mean that? About cooking me dinner and sucking my dick, or was that just in-the-moment talk?"

Julian's eyes went as wide as his grin. "I don't recall saying the dick-sucking part."

"You said you wanted to taste more of me. I just assumed . . ."

He cupped my face in both his hands and kissed me again. "That's exactly what I meant. And yes, dinner too, if you want."

"Oh, I want."

He closed his eyes, his forehead against mine. "God, tell me to leave. I don't want to go, but if I don't go now, I will take you to bed."

"Well, that's not a very good argument for me to tell you to leave."

He groaned out a laugh. "Malachi, I'm trying to pace this. I want to do everything to you, with you, but I don't want to go too fast in case we burn out. I haven't felt like this in so long. I'm trying to take it slow and do the right thing."

I kissed him, soft and sweet. "I want to do everything with you too," I whispered. His eyes were brown-and-gold galaxies. "So dinner tomorrow night sounds lovely. And we can have all the usual dating conversations, like favourite movies and books. And we can talk about families and friends and embarrassing childhood stories, our first times, and all the things you want to know about me." I pecked his lips with mine. "And then you can do all the tasting of my dick you want."

Julian hummed. "And you can taste mine."

"Sure. I'll just unhinge my jaw like a snake so it fits."

He scoffed at that. "Okay, so I'm not *that* big."

"Fear not, good man," I proclaimed boldly. "I spent my later teen years devouring giant all-day suckers in preparation for this moment. It's my time to shine."

He laughed, his whole face so damn happy. "I should go. Thank you for tonight."

"My pleasure. Literally. And thank you for dinner."

"You're welcome. Oh, my shirt . . ."

"I'll bring it with me to your place tomorrow night. Text me your address and I'll book an Uber. What time should I arrive?"

"I'll pick you up around six thirty," he replied. Then he took my chin in between his thumb and forefinger and kissed me. "Like a proper date. I'll pick you up, feed you, take care of you, and drop you home whenever you want. I want to treat you right, Malachi."

"Sounds good." It sounded better than good. It sounded great.

With a soft, lingering kiss, he left. And I cleaned up a bit, let a disgruntled Buster Jones in from the balcony for his nightly squander of free food, and I went to bed feeling all floaty.

I was happy.

On that new-romance buzz, the thrill and excitement of every look, of every touch. He was different to any guy I'd ever been with. He was genuine and lovely and kind. He totally had a bit of a daddy vibe, which suited me just fine. After all, I was a twenty-seven-year-old twinky man-boy that probably needed looking after more than I wanted to admit.

I wanted him to look after me.

His strong arms, his gentle touch. To eat dinner with me, to watch TV with me, to laugh and talk with me, then to whisper in my ear all the filthy things he wanted to do to me. God, I wanted that. I wanted him to use my body like a sex toy. *He* was what I wanted.

Yeah, I was happy.

I told myself it was too early for love.

I couldn't call it love.

It was lust and infatuation, excitement and butterflies.

It was far too soon for love.

Wasn't it?

WASN'T IT?

CHAPTER FOURTEEN

"MORNING!" I said brightly as I entered the breakroom. Paul and Theo were at their usual table, Paul with his newspaper and Theo talking to him regardless. Denise was at the kitchenette making herself a cuppa, and Cherry was sitting at her table reading something on her phone.

They all replied good morning in some variation. I quickly made my coffee and joined Denise and Cherry. "So," I began, "if I needed to try and find the class records of a high school in the 60s or 70s, how would I go about doing that? Social media groups for that school aren't public, and I found nothing on any of the three dozen websites that have school photos from the olden days."

"The olden days?" Paul asked. "You'd probably need to contact the National Historical Society for any photos from the 1870s."

I turned around to face their table. He and Theo were both staring at me. I hadn't intended for this to be a whole squad conversation but it was too late.

"Uh, I meant the 1960s and 1970s," I explained.

Paul blinked. "The 70s are the olden days?"

Oh fuck.

"I drove a Ford Charger in the 70s, not a horse and carriage, son."

"I didn't mean . . ." I shrugged. "Well actually, I did mean the olden days because . . ."

Paul raised one serial-killer eyebrow.

"You know what?" I quickly changed tack. "I'm good. I'll find it, I'm sure."

"You could try calling the school. They keep old year-books forever," Theo suggested. "Or the local library might have copies. If it were me, I'd call the closest library and just explain what you're after. Librarians love info retrieval missions. It's like adding a Zelda side-quest to their day. Seriously, call them."

I smiled at the Zelda comment.

"That's a good idea, thanks."

"Is this for your secret squirrel stuff?" Paul asked. He seemed to have gotten over the olden day reference.

"Ah, yes."

"I love secret squirrel stuff," Denise said, excited. "What's it about?"

"Well, I can't tell you that," I replied. "Then it wouldn't be secret squirrel stuff."

"He's looking into the Milton James letters for me," Julian replied from the doorway. His deep voice both excited and soothed me.

I spun to see him smiling at me. He was wearing brown again, though this time there was a dark umber knitted vest, no tie, his shirt sleeves rolled just once.

It might have been a contender for the sexiest school-teacher outfit, if there were awards for such things. Which there totally should be, because he would win. Was he a teacher? No. Did he look like one? Yes. Did I want afternoon detention with him? Hell yes. I would even argue that maybe he could bring back the cane just so he'd spank me . . .

I hadn't realised everyone was now looking at me, because I was still staring at Julian.

Did he just . . . did he just tell them what I was working on?

He walked in, giving me a smile as he went past on his way to make himself a coffee. "I decided we should try finding the sender or the recipient of the Milton James letters, and I asked Malachi to do it."

Everyone's eyes went from Julian back to me, but Julian continued to explain. "I asked him not to tell anyone, so don't blame him. I just felt, given the sensitive nature of the letters, that privacy would be best. It wasn't anything against anyone else here. I just wanted to respect their . . . secret."

"They're gay?" Paul asked. "Because you know we don't care about none of that."

Julian's cheeks tinged pink and he glanced at me before he focused on Paul. "I know that, thank you." He cleared his throat. "I just . . . I just assumed Malachi and I would be best suited to assess them."

I held my fist up. "Gay Avengers unite."

Denise cleared her throat. "Uh, excuse me. What am I? I'm totally a gay Avenger. I might look more like Thor, but can I please be Black Widow? She's smoking hot."

Cherry waved. "I'm an honorary gay Avenger, considering I helped already. I'll be Scarlett Witch for this exercise."

"Ooh," Theo said, standing up. "I'll be Magneto."

"He's X-Men," I said.

"That's okay," Julian said gently. "Magneto's fine."

This was getting bizarre, but we all looked at Paul, waiting for him to pick an Avenger. He rolled his eyes. "I'll be . . ."

If he says Thanos . . .

"Thanos."

I fucking knew it.

"Of course," I replied. "Good choice."

It was not a good choice. It was the worst choice.

"So now we're all honorary gay Avengers," Theo said. "Can we help?"

"What about Glenda?" Denise said. Everyone turned to look at the shrine of the dead woman, ex-employee, on the wall. "Pretty sure she'd have liked to be an Avenger."

I tried to think if there were any accordion-playing, cat-loving Avengers. I couldn't think of any . . .

Paul and Cherry answered at the same time. "Groot."

Theo said, "Storm!"

I was going to have to give him a rundown on the differences between X-Men and Marvel.

"I think Groot is fair," Julian said, giving me a smile.

Jesus. So Glenda was a cat-loving, accordion-playing octogenarian woman who could speak just three words. "I wish I'd have met her," I said because, honestly, she sounded awesome.

"Who are you going to be?" Theo asked me.

Oh. Me . . . "Um—"

"Loki," Cherry, Paul, and Denise all answered in unison.

I was stunned and affronted, but mostly proud. Julian smiled at me. "And what about you?" I asked him. "Which Avenger are you?"

He tilted his head to think. "I'm not sure."

"Steve Rogers," Paul answered.

"Peter Parker," Denise offered.

Cherry studied him for a second. "Tony Stark."

"Wolverine!" Theo yelled proudly. We all ignored him.

Julian nodded slowly. "It is duly noted that I'm the boring human counterpart of the Avenger heroes and not their superhero persona." He sipped his coffee. "I can accept that."

I laughed. "Well, I have a list of notes I've taken from the letters, if anyone's interested in helping. The only thing I've found are dead ends." I took my list from my pocket. "I have school information."

"For the olden days," Paul deadpanned.

I nodded and smiled at him. "Correct. So maybe school records or a local library might help, as Theo said."

"Me!" Theo yelled so loud poor Denise almost dropped her coffee. "I can do that."

"Okay, thanks," I replied. "And I have a possible military lead, if we can access some dates for Duntroon."

Denise and Theo both pointed to Paul, and Paul gave a shrug. "I have connections."

I honestly should have guessed that.

"What about me?" Denise asked. "I'm not just the fork-lift driver. I can look for stuff."

I handed her the list. "Take a pick."

She read through it and gave a nod. "I'll have a think."

"Excellent." This was actually exciting. I didn't even mind handing tasks off if it meant we would have an answer sooner. "I've tried searching at home, just with Google, but it wasn't much help."

Paul and Theo took my notes to their desks to start whatever it was they were going to do, and then the back loading dock buzzer went off. "Well, that's me," Denise said, disappearing out the door.

Cherry made herself another coffee and gave me and Julian a nod as she zipped out the door, and that left just Julian and me.

"Sorry if you didn't want me to tell them," he said gently. "I just hated that you might have to had lied."

"No apologies necessary. I'm happy they know. Now they can do all the searching and I can get my carts unloaded quicker. Then I'll help them do theirs. Plus, they're so much better at finding information than me."

"I think you're doing pretty great," he murmured. "You have a success rate similar to everyone else at putting the mail back into circulation."

I stood up and washed my coffee cup. "Thank you."

He came to stand beside me, washing his cup as I dried mine. "Are we still on for tonight?"

"Hell yes, we are," I answered. "Oh, and as for which Avenger you are. You are one hundred per cent the Hulk."

He met my eyes. "The Hulk?"

"Yep. I've seen you naked. Definitely been some gamma radiation happening there. It makes everything really big, if you know what I mean."

He cleared his throat. "Yes, I get it. And I probably should thank you for not saying that in front of the others."

I grinned. "You're welcome. Anyway, I better get to work before I get Hulk-smashed." Then I stopped. "Actually, getting Hulk-smashed by your huge—"

"Okay, thanks, Malachi. There will be no smashing."

I gave him a wink. "Not until after dinner, anyway."

He was still smiling as I walked out.

I WOULD NEVER BE one to toot my own horn . . . *Who am I kidding? I talk myself up all the time.* But I kicked arse at work. I ran cages, I filed letters, parcels, boxes, crates, and canisters. I did my own, then put a dent in everyone else's workload because they were helping me.

I saw Paul on the phone a few times, writing down notes, clicking away at his keyboard. Theo was the same, and I was certain I heard him on the phone flirting with a librarian in Milldale.

I was a little proud.

Denise had a skip in her step and told me she'd put in a few calls. Cherry smiled at me every time she saw me, which, for a goth girl, was like winning the lottery.

There was a definite vibe in the air. Like a buzz that we were all on the same mission.

Like a team.

By the end of the day, though, it was only Paul who had something back for his efforts.

"Malachi," he said, calling me over, holding up a notepad. "This is all I could get. Between my contact and public records, I have four names. There were six, but two signed up voluntarily so I excluded them. These four men were registered in the army from the local Milldale shire after the conscription. Aged between eighteen and twenty, all went to Duntroon. I searched through the Vietnam War records of Australian involvement and found this guy, Peter Digby, was involved in a battle on the Laos border, so if you say your guy never left the country, I think we can put a line through him. This guy, Steven Harrell." He pointed to his list. "His entire record is basically redacted."

"What does that mean?" I asked.

"Well," Paul said thoughtfully. "My guess is he did a lot of shit the government doesn't want anyone to know about.

Covert ops, retrievals, murders. That kind of thing. There were a lot of covert ops during the war, a lot of under-the-table deals that the public doesn't know about."

I didn't want to know how he knew this kind of stuff. "Nice."

Paul didn't seem fazed at all. "Anyhoo, that means he very likely saw action overseas, so we can cross him out. So that leaves these two. Michael Flannagan and Errol Hunt." He ripped out the piece of paper and handed it to me.

I had two names.

"Oh my god," I whispered. "Thank you."

Paul shrugged but I could tell he was kinda proud. "It's not exact, and there's always room for error. But by process of elimination, I narrowed it down for ya. It's a place to start, anyway."

I nodded. "It is. Thank you."

Julian came out of his office and I held up the list to show him. "We have two names for the guy who went to Duntroon. He could be one of these two. Paul narrowed it down. Now I just need to search up Michael and Errol to see if they returned to the Milldale area. This could be a real possible lead."

"That's awesome," Julian said, but I could tell by his tone that he wanted to say something but not in front of the others. I could ask him about it later because this sexy man was making me dinner tonight, amongst other things he was going to do for me. Or to me, to be specific.

I checked my watch. "Shoot. It's almost five."

"You in a rush today?" Paul asked. "You've been running around like a blue-arsed fly all day."

"Can't miss the bus," I said, folding the piece of paper and slipping it into my pocket.

"Ooh, got a hot date?" Paul went on. He very obviously

meant it as a joke, and there was no way he could have known about me and Julian. He was just being himself and saying cringy things.

But I decided to play along. "I have a scorching hot date tonight." I deliberately didn't make eye contact with Julian. "I have a lot to do before he picks me up for dinner, so I can't be late." I could have explained the douching process but doubted Paul or Theo would enjoy the details. I went to my computer and turned it off, beginning to pack up my desk.

"I got Susan's phone number," Theo announced, standing up proudly. "The librarian at Milldale."

I stood up so I could see him over the cubicle wall. "You did?"

He looked so proud he could burst. He held up a slip of paper. "Yep. We got talking and she was nice, so I asked her for her number and she got all giggly and gave it to me."

Well, I'll be damned. "Look at you go!"

He grinned, his cheeks pink. "She likes sudoku and making papier- mâché."

Well, that was random as hell, but okay. "Awesome."

"She's going to look through all the yearbooks for anyone called Raymond and call me back." He was so happy, I wanted to squish his chubby cheeks.

"Oh hey, you're all here. Got some info for ya's," Denise said, walking out one of the aisles. She had her phone pressed to her ear. "Okay, Doll . . . you're a national treasure . . . yes, I'm sure. See you then," she said into the phone, then disconnected the call. She looked at me, then Julian. "If you wanna know anything about gay history in this city, you ask the elders, right? So I called old Dolly. She's been on the lesbian scene forever. She'd have to be seventy by now. Can still knock a smartarse off a barstool though, but that's a different story for another time. Anyway, I called her and asked her if she's heard the name Milton James. It was a long shot, but it had to mean something, right?"

This was taking forever and I had a bus to catch. "And?"

Denise obviously liked to tell stories. "So the gay scene in the late sixties and early seventies was mostly underground because cops would raid clubs and arrest anyone who even looked remotely gay, right?"

God.

Julian nodded. "Right."

"So there was a community radio station back then on some random AM frequency that was run out of a room above a pub on Oxford Street. They'd announce all kinds of stuff, most of it in code so the cops wouldn't be able to figure it out, like decoy addresses for parties, that kind of thing."

"Okay," I said, trying to prompt her along.

"And there was a segment on the radio one night a week called *Dearest Milton James*."

I felt the blood run from my face.

I shot Julian a look. "Dearest Milton James."

He looked as stunned as me. He turned, wide-eyed, back to Denise. "What else did she say?"

"It was like a talkback program, but you could write in. He'd answer any questions about sex or dating. He'd also read erotic poetry. Or whatever people wrote in, he'd read on-air. They had a postbox, but it only lasted a year until the cops waited for someone to collect the mail and that put an end to it."

"Oh my god," I whispered.

Denise nodded. "Dolly might be old, but she's as sharp as they come. She never forgets a thing. She knows every single thing that went on back then."

"He was writing to a radio show," I mumbled, sitting down at my desk. "They must have listened to the show. Well, Raymond definitely did but I wonder if they listened together. Maybe they drove out to the river and listened in the car? I don't know. But Raymond wanted the radio guy to read the letters on-air, but they never made it."

Paul tapped his watch. "You'll miss your bus."

"There'll be another one," I whispered. Why did this hurt so much? Why did finding out this information make me feel terrible. "*Dearest Milton James* was a radio segment for gay people so they could communicate and share stories."

Denise came over and put her hand on my shoulder, giving me a bit of a shake. "It's a good thing. Folks back then found ways around the laws to make themselves a community. Just shows how resilient they were back then. How they would always rise above it."

I nodded. When she put it like that . . . "I suppose."

"You ready, Malachi?" Cherry had collected her bag and she glanced at the clock. "I'll walk to the bus with you."

"Yeah, sure," I said. "Thank you, everyone, for helping. You guys are the best. I never would have found this stuff out on my own."

Everyone acted like it was no big deal, even if it was, and they began packing up as I walked to the door with Cherry. Except for Julian, who was watching me, clearly wanting to speak with me, probably ask why I was catching the bus but not sure how to without being obvious.

I took my phone out of my pocket and shot him a quick message as I got to the door.

Six thirty. Don't be late.

I held the door open for Cherry and turned back to see Julian smiling at his phone.

CHAPTER FIFTEEN

AT 6.25 I got a text message from Julian.

I'm parked out front. Want me to come up?

I was going to reply but figured it'd be quicker if I just went to meet him. He didn't need to know I'd been showered, dressed and ready for ages, counting down the minutes.

I found his car and he got out when he saw me. Walking around to the passenger side, he held my door open. "Good evening," he said. "You look amazing."

I'd put a bright orange dye over the fading purple streak in my otherwise jet-black hair. I wore tight black jeans with a vintage Guns N' Roses shirt with the orange cross. I had bright orange ribbon laces in my Docs.

"Thank you. You're as sexy as ever," I replied, getting in his car. He closed the door and smiled at me the whole way around to his side.

"You changed your hair," he said as he climbed in behind the wheel.

"It's conveniently coincidental that it takes the same

amount of time to dye my hair as it does to douche. I can multitask."

He stared, then burst out laughing. "Okay then."

"I wasn't sure it would be required, but I didn't want to regret not doing it. You did say you wanted to taste all of me, and I didn't know if you liked to eat arse, but I like to be prepared."

He made a fucking hot grunting sound as he shifted in his seat. "Christ, Malachi."

His reaction made me preen a little. "Sorry."

I was not sorry. We both knew it.

He pulled the car out onto the street, reached over the console and took my hand, sending a rush of warmth through me. "You feeling okay about today? Finding out about who Milton James was?" he asked.

I gave him a smile. "I feel better now, yes. What Denise said was right. They did find a way to be themselves and create their own community. I don't know why I was so bummed when I first heard it. I just thought it was sad, but it was a different time. I can't imagine . . . I guess it was just a good reminder of how lucky I have it." I squeezed his hand. "I've been out since I was like nine. It was never a big deal. I was a disappointment to my parents in school, at work, never went to college, got fired for wearing a skirt. So my gayness was probably a relief, to be honest. There was no risk of me being even more of a disappointment by impregnating girls all over town."

Julian chuckled. "You mentioned siblings, yes?"

"An older brother and sister. They're responsible and very heterosexual with their office jobs, picket fences, and 2.5 children, so all expectations landed on them. I'm the rainbow sheep of the family that gets to run loose in the top paddock." I couldn't believe we'd never really discussed our families before. "What about you?"

"I have two sisters, one older, one younger. My younger sister is bisexual, currently seeing a guy for about two years now. And my older sister is actually an ordained minister, if you could believe that. And she's a foster mum. Has a brood with her at all times and is so busy, I'm positive she never sleeps."

"Wow."

He shot me a smile. "My parents have always accepted us as we are. Never questioned our decisions, just want us to be happy. My dad was a plumber until he hurt his back a few years ago. He's okay now, but it laid him out for a while, and he took it as a sign to retire early so he sold his business. My mum is an accountant. They live in Ashfield, in the house I grew up in."

"I love that." Then I made a face. "Well, I don't really need to tell you about my dad because you know him. Even though you told him I was your sexiest employee the other day."

He laughed. "You know I didn't actually say that."

"What did you tell him?"

"He just asked how you were settling in. I said you were a great asset to the team and you fit in really well."

"Was he surprised?"

Julian squeezed my fingers and left my hand on his thigh while he used two hands to drive. We'd turned off into a nice-looking residential street. "I don't think so."

"Speaking of team," I mused. "I think telling everyone about the Milton James letters and deciding to find who this Raymond is was a good idea. Everyone was involved and they seemed really happy about that."

"I noticed that too. There was a different mood at work today."

"Like a team."

Julian nodded. "Yeah. It was nice, actually."

"Maybe every so often we could take an old case and do a team job on solving it. Like once a month or something."

Julian smiled at me. "I like that idea." He slowed the car and reverse parallel parked like a pro, then shut off the engine. "Well, we're here."

The street was lined with narrow two-storey town-houses, some with little porches and fences, some with plants and flowers. It was gorgeous. "You live in a townhouse?"

"I do. It's small and very narrow."

Then a horrific thought occurred. "Oh my god, do you have housemates? Am I meeting strange people in the next ten seconds? Because I'm not mentally prepared."

Julian laughed. "No, I live alone. I would've given you plenty of warning before now if that was the case."

The relief was instantaneous. Plus, I wasn't up for sexy times with an audience.

We got out of his car and I followed him up to his door. His townhouse was a slate grey colour with a black wrought iron fence, gate, and window trim. It was lovely. Inside was a living room first, very narrow, like he'd said. But it was light with tall ceilings. His furniture was well chosen for the room, nothing cluttered, very trendy gay. The living room backed onto a kitchen, which was relatively new, also white and very tidy. He didn't offer me a tour of upstairs, and I didn't ask; I figured I'd see his bed later.

"Your place is beautiful," I said. "Very grown-up. Makes my retro vintage seem rather childish."

He chuckled. "Your place is very you."

"What, childish? Or second-hand and cheap?"

He laughed. "Not like that. I meant bright, colourful, and lots of fun." Then he took my hand and turned me a little before backing me up to the kitchen counter. He pressed against me, lifting my chin so he could kiss me, soft and warm and lingering. "I've wanted to do that all day," he murmured before kissing me again.

There was no urgency, no rush, as if he wanted to savour every second. Like he wanted me to feel his tenderness and his honesty. Like he felt the same about me as I felt about him.

Like he knew this didn't make sense, that it was all too fast, that we shouldn't feel like this after so little time.

Eventually he ended the kiss and rested his forehead on mine. "So . . . dinner."

"So, dinner," I repeated in a whisper. I was ready to say fuck dinner, let's go to bed.

"Ugh," he said, taking a step back. "I'm trying to do the right thing here. As in, a proper date."

"You're doing a very good job."

He shook his head and laughed. "So I thought I would try something new and I found a spicy Thai noodle dish that looked great, but then I panicked and I called Curtis, my friend. Anyway, I told him I wanted to impress you and he said to make you my linguine dish. So that's what I went with. I had to get fresh linguine from the deli on the way home and Italian sausage and the proper ricotta."

"Well, it sounds amazing . . . but you wanted to impress me? And you told your friend about me?"

He grinned and started taking ingredients out of the fridge, putting them on the counter. "Of course I did." He met my eyes. "You said you told your friends about me."

"Well, one friend. Moni. And yes, of course, I tell her

everything. And I mean everything." Then I rolled my eyes. "You don't need to impress me. I'm already impressed."

He smiled, blushing faintly. "Okay, so this dish takes no time at all. Did you want to help me slice and dice stuff, or did you want to pull a chair into the kitchen, sip on a glass of wine, and look pretty while you supervise?"

"I'm totally going to supervise. And look pretty, of course, but you just gave me the option to sit here and ogle you. That's a no-contest, my guy." I pulled a chair over, like he said, and sat at the edge of the kitchen. He poured two glasses of red wine and handed me one. "And," I continued, "you don't want me to help with cooking. I have many talents, however, cooking is not one of them."

"Looking pretty is, though," he said. "You do it so well."

"I know. It's a burden sometimes."

He chuckled, then began to chop and dice, looking all kinds of relaxed and gorgeous moving around his kitchen. He fried and simmered stuff and the aromas were making my stomach growl.

But there was something I wanted to ask. "Can I ask you something?"

"Sure."

"Today, when Paul had reduced the Duntroon list of names to two and I mentioned maybe contacting them, the look on your face told me you didn't think that was a great idea."

"Well . . ."

"Well what?"

He sighed and sounded apologetic. He stopped chopping and turned to me. "You can't just call someone up out of the blue and say, 'Hey, were you in an intimate relationship with a guy called Raymond in the 70s?'. He could be married with grandkids and doesn't want anyone to know about that time in his life. It could be damaging for him."

My heart sank. "I know, and that's a fair call. I'd need to do more research first. And once we've gathered all the info we can find and we're pretty certain it's the right guy, we'll make an informed decision then, if we contact him at all. I wouldn't just drop a bombshell for my curiosity's sake."

Julian gave me a soft smile. "I think our only point of contact should be Raymond."

I sipped my wine and let him explain.

"For all we know, the guy he wrote about doesn't even know the letters exist. And maybe they're completely fictional. They don't read like they are. Everything he talks about feels real, but how do we know? He could have been writing a story to make it seem real, just to be read out on the radio like it was a real relationship. Like a radio serial story. He mentioned going to uni for English, so maybe he liked to write stories. We just don't know."

"I hadn't thought of that."

Julian sighed. "I want it to be real. I want there to be some kind of happy ending, but . . ." He shrugged. "We just don't know."

"That's a fair call," I allowed.

He turned back to his chopping board and scraped the diced greens into the pan. "Can I be totally honest with you?"

Oh god. "Yeah, of course. Although that pre-empt never ends well, but sure."

He chuckled and leaned his hip against the counter. "Don't be mad at me."

"Oh, for fuck sake, Julian, are you married?"

"What? No!"

"Straight?"

"Definitely not."

"Seeing someone else?"

"Not at all."

"Then I won't be mad. Unless you're the type of person who pours the milk in before the cereal."

"Who does that?"

"Heathens."

He laughed. "No, it's nothing like that." He took a deep breath. "Okay, here goes. When I asked you to help me look into these letters, I didn't think we'd ever find the person who wrote them, or who he sent them to or who Dearest Milton James was. I didn't think we'd ever find them. They were old and so vague, and there was no address, no real names, no anything."

Uh, what . . . ?

"Then why did you suggest—"

"I needed an excuse to spend time with you. I wanted to see you outside of work and I was too gutless to just ask."

"Oh."

"I'm so sorry. It was never my intent to deceive you. I just didn't know how to ask you out without giving myself hives. And then you actually began to find information and it was exciting. And for the record, I'm glad we're finding them. I'm glad we have all these leads. If we can return the letters to Raymond, then that'll be awesome. I just never thought we would." He put his hand to his forehead. "I'm sorry."

I couldn't help it. I laughed. "What are you sorry for? That's kind of sweet. You certainly didn't lie. You told me you thought we should try to find them. And we did try. That's not lying." I got off the stool and went to him, cupping his face in my hand. "I'm glad you asked me, and

I'm glad we spent time together outside of work. I just think it's funny that you were too nervous to ask."

"I wasn't lying when I said I've been out of the game for a while. Everything I've told you is the truth. I like you, and I want to keep seeing you. And I do want to find this Raymond guy and return the letters to him. I just never thought we would."

I leaned up on my toes and kissed him softly. "I like you too, and I want to keep seeing you. And I'd be a big fat liar if I said I didn't agree to help you find him just to be able to spend more time with you. Though I had visions of us staying back in your office and having super-hot desk sex, but dinner dates are also fun."

Julian chuckled and pulled me in for a proper kiss, his arms around my back, holding me close while he deepened the kiss.

Until my stomach growled, and he broke away with a laugh. "Okay, I will feed you first."

I was torn between being starving hungry and horny. "Sorry, apparently my stomach approves of your cooking. It smells so good."

Ten minutes later, we were sitting at his dining table eating the best pasta I'd ever tasted in my life. I considered licking the empty plate but thought I'd better not. "Please thank Curtis for suggesting you cook this. I'm more than impressed, and now the bad news for you is that I will expect this level of brilliance every time you cook for me."

Julian laughed, pushed his plate away, then sipped his wine. "I'd like to take the credit, but honestly, the Italian deli I get the ingredients from makes it impossible to taste bad. They make the pasta themselves, it takes five minutes to cook. And they import the sausage and ricotta direct from

Italy, and I'm pretty sure the vine-ripened tomatoes are grown out the back of the store."

I chuckled. "Well, thank them for me too. This was delicious."

"I'm glad you enjoyed it. Though I didn't get anything for dessert. I can offer you more wine. Or an espresso?"

"Or you could make dessert out of me and take me to your bedroom."

His gaze shot to mine; he had fire in his eyes. "Malachi," he breathed.

He wanted me as much as I wanted him. There was no denying it. And I'd always been upfront about what I wanted.

And I wanted him.

I pushed my chair out and stood, going to him. I lifted my leg and straddled him, sitting on his lap, on his crotch. He was still sitting at the table, so it was kind of crowded, but he quickly put his arms around me and looked up to my face. "You're very bold."

I rocked forward a little, grinding on him. I slid my arms around his neck and kissed him. If he was hesitant at all, it melted away as soon as my tongue touched his. He groaned in my mouth and tightened his arms around me.

I could feel his hardening dick as he pulled me closer, kissed me deeper.

"I have my last STI test results in a text message on my phone," I whispered, desperate. "I am good to go."

He inhaled deeply and put his forehead on my chin and caught his breath. When he looked up at me, his eyes were sharp and dark. "I was tested for everything after my ex . . . I haven't been with anyone since."

"No one?" He shook his head, and I smiled. "Then you must really want to come so bad."

He stood so quick I thought he was dumping me off his lap, but he held onto my arse and lifted me with him.

Oh, hell yes.

Never breaking eye contact, he slowly lowered me to the floor, keeping me pulled close. "I want you," he whispered. I thought my knees might buckle, but he took my hand and led the way up the stairs. His room was long and narrow. His bed looked huge and soft, the covers light grey. There were books on his bedside table but I didn't have time to read the spines because he pushed me onto his bed and crawled on after me.

He prowled up my body, between my legs and undid my button and fly.

Holy fuck.

He freed my cock from my briefs and, locking eyes with me, he leaned down and licked me. He ran his flattened tongue right up the shaft, tongued the head, then took me into his mouth. Just for a taste, because he pulled off and sat back. I was about to protest when he began to pull my jeans off, then my shirt.

"Want you naked," he said.

"You too," I said. My voice sounded like I'd smoked two packs of cigarettes a day for sixty years. It made him smile but he unbuttoned his shirt and popped the buttons on his pants like a fucking porn star. I had to squeeze my dick to stave off my orgasm.

I was so ready for this.

He smiled as he gripped my base and took me back into his mouth, sucking, swirling, licking, pumping, and fingering my balls.

Fuck.

"Julian," I murmured. "I'm close already."

So of course he grunted and took me into his throat, and

that was the final push. I gripped his bed covers and tumbled over the edge, coming down his throat.

My entire body convulsed, and he sucked every drop out of me.

"Gawd."

He hummed and pulled off, smiling, victorious. Then lifted me like I was a paper doll, leaning me against the padded headboard. He straddled my chest, took his huge fucking cock in his fist, and I certainly didn't need telling to open my mouth.

There was no way I could take him all, not even close. But I worked the head of his cock like a Chupa Chup, and I was rewarded for my efforts. He was so hard and swollen, and he grunted and cussed when he came, gripping the headboard as he pulsed in my mouth.

I had to wonder how much self-control it took not to thrust into my throat.

When his orgasm had run its course, he pulled back and manoeuvred me down the bed a little so he could wrap his arms around me. It might have been the best thing ever.

But then snoozing became snogging and more kissing became mutual hand jobs, and it was around midnight when we went downstairs for a snack.

"I guess I should go home," I said. "But I'll call an Uber. You don't need to drive me."

He stepped closer and fed me a cracker with cheese. He thumbed a crumb off. "Or you could stay."

He chuckled at my very surprised expression. I forgot to chew the cracker and tried to speak. "Uhmff?"

"Stay." He laughed again, tracing his fingers through my hair. "I can drive you past your place on the way to work tomorrow morning if you need anything. Stay tonight." He kissed me again. "In my bed."

CHAPTER SIXTEEN

WAKING up in Julian's bed, in his arms, was surreal. Being the little spoon to him was warm and safe, and his bed was ten times better than mine, so I could also add luxurious to the list of superfluous adverbs in my floaty brain.

For a brief second, I'd thought I'd woken up in heaven.

His huge morning wood didn't help . . . Actually, could that be called a trunk? Or a log? A branch didn't seem right . . .

"Morning," he murmured, voice deep and rough. He kissed the back of my head.

"Hmm." I sighed. "Brain isn't fully functional yet."

He ran his hand down my side, over my hip, and he chuckled. "Want me to help with that?"

God, yes.

I wiggled my arse as my answer, trying to line up his erection between my arse cheeks. His firm hand on my hip stilled me. "Is that a yes?"

"Yes, please."

So he got up on his knees, pulled my legs over his thighs, bringing me close. I thought for a second he was going to fuck me, but he slid our shafts together, pressed together in his fist, and began to jerk us both off.

I think I lasted maybe twenty seconds. Twenty-five, tops. He came straight after me, jerking off onto my belly. His strong body, his skilful touch, his perfect cock, and the sounds he made when he came . . .

So fucking hot.

He collapsed on top of me and I wanted to stay there forever. With his weight on me, his come smeared on me.

I never wanted to leave.

"I'll fall asleep if you keep rubbing circles on my back," he mumbled.

I hummed happily. "Do you think they'd miss us if we both called in sick today?"

Julian laughed into my neck, making me shiver. "I think they would, yes."

"Such a shame."

Julian rolled us over. "Shower time. You first."

"Are we not showering together?"

"If we do that, we won't be going to work today."

"That's not helping your argument."

He chuckled again and, taking my hand, helped me off the bed. He showed me into his bathroom, offered me a huge fluffy towel, and left me to it. His shower was bigger than mine, the water hotter. Everything in his place was better than mine. But not wanting to use all his hot water, I made it quick.

He, of course, was downstairs. Coffee and toast was made. He took one look at me wearing my clothes from last night. "We can run past your place on the way to work if you want," he offered.

"Nope, it's fine. I only had them on for about two hours. But just so you know, I'm not wearing my briefs. I am totally free-balling it right now, so all day at work you'll have the privilege of knowing I'm not wearing any underpants."

He made a low grunt sound. "That's not fair."

I sipped my coffee. "Just something for you to think about all day before you make good on your promise for tonight."

He closed his eyes slowly and put his coffee down. He let out a slow, measured breath. "Okay. I should go shower. Before we don't go to work today."

I grinned as he glowered at me when he trudged up the stairs. I had to wonder how much I could tease him before he threw me down on the bed and taught me a lesson.

I had no clue how strong his resolve was, but I was keen to find out.

I took a bite of my toast just as my phone beeped. It was a message from Moni.

If you don't reply to this text I'll call the police.

It was apparently the third text she'd sent me. Two late last night and now this one. She was checking up on me after my date to make sure I was okay.

I hit Call.

"Are you dead?"

"Been to heaven a few times, but nope, still on this mortal coil."

"I texted you last night."

"Sorry. I was busy going to heaven."

She laughed. "Well, I'm glad to hear that. You must have got home late."

"I'm still at his place."

"You are?"

"Yep. He's in the shower. He cooked me dinner last night; he made me breakfast this morning. Moni, he's the sweetest man I've ever been with."

"Aww."

"And hung. He's hung, Moni. Like those slab sticks of salami in a deli window. My arse may never be the same, and I cannot fucking wait."

"So you didn't go that far yet?"

"Not yet. Tonight, probably."

"Well, be safe."

"Always."

"Text me if you need."

"I will. And same. If you go out tonight and need me, you call."

"I wouldn't dare interrupt your slab-of-salami dick sex."

I snorted. "I will forgo even that for you."

"Liar."

"Love you."

"Love you too. Have fun tonight."

"Oh, I will."

She laughed and hung up on me, so I finished my toast and washed up the few things we'd used. I was drying them when Julian came downstairs. He wore his navy pants, a sky-blue button-down shirt with a smile on his face and a skip in his step.

He took my breath away.

"Good morning, handsome," I said, giving him a blatant once over.

He fixed his glasses and blushed. "Are you ready?"

"Sure am."

Morning traffic was shit, as always, and the drive was slow. Not that I minded. Julian would give me smiley side-eyes every so often, and I was so fucking happy and stupidly giddy, I could have burst.

"So, this afternoon," I said. "I can catch the bus home

like I did yesterday. That way people won't think it's suspicious if we leave together."

Julian made a thoughtful face. "Well, you can catch the bus if you want. I don't mind either way. But there's a good chance someone will see you getting out of my car this morning, which is probably harder to explain, so . . ."

"Oh shit. Did you want to drop me off down the block and I can walk up?"

He laughed. "No. I'm not dropping you off halfway down the block. If they see us, they see." He shrugged. "Unless you don't want to? If you're not comfortable—"

"No, I just don't want it to cause problems, that's all."

He squeezed my thigh and I threaded our fingers together on my knee. "How about we just take it one day at a time," he said. "If they ask questions, we'll answer them. No need to lie." He was quiet for a few minutes. "Can I ask you something?"

"Sure."

"What do you think your father would say if or when he finds out?"

I smiled at him. "Are you asking as my boss or as a potential boyfriend?"

He rolled his eyes, but the flush of colour down his cheeks gave him away. "Both, I guess. Either. Both."

"As my boss, he can't really say anything. It's not a breach of any protocol or regulations. He might not like it, but he introduced us so it's his fault. As a potential boyfriend, you have a great job and you treat me well, so he has to like you. Also, he introduced us, so it's his fault."

Julian laughed. "I'm sure he'd really enjoy being told that."

I grinned at him. "So . . . have you been considering this potential boyfriend thing for long?"

He shook his head, smiling. "I'm not answering that. There is no right answer and anything I say can be used against me."

I laughed. "But you have considered it."

He refused to answer, choosing to turn up the music instead. But that was fine. Because he had considered it . . .

I grinned all the way to work.

WE WERE the first ones there, which was probably a good thing. And if any of them thought it was weird that I was in the breakroom before them, no one mentioned it.

Well, Cherry might have given me a side-eye but she knew about me and Julian anyway, so thankfully, she chose not to bring it up.

Theo talked non-stop about his phone conversation with his Milldale librarian friend. Though she had retrieved the yearbooks from the archives, she hadn't had a chance to look through them yet. It was on her to-do list for today.

So we had to wait.

I found getting through as much inventory as I could was a good way to pass the time. It worked as a distraction at least. I didn't see Theo at his desk much, he was busy running his cage as well, and I told myself these letters had waited forty-something years, another day wouldn't hurt.

The librarian would get back to him when she could . . .

I managed a quick bite at lunch and got straight back to work, and I was at the bottom of the J-K aisle when Theo yelled out my name so loud I could only guess that he'd either heard back from his librarian or the building was on fire.

I raced up to the front to find him excitedly waving a piece of paper in the air. "I have something!"

I was so excited my hands were shaking. Or maybe that was because I actually ran and my body was in shock. "What is it?"

"From 1969 to 1973 there were four Raymond's who went to Northbury High," he said. Then he brought up some images on his computer. "Susan scanned the pages for me. Raymond Bing was in fourth form in 1969. He played rugby for the school. Raymond Allcott was in sixth form in 1970. Says here the school wished him well at medical school, for which he was already accepted." Theo shrugged. "I think we can forget those two." He pulled up another image. "This is Raymond Dunn. He graduated in 1972. Excelled in English and drama club. Was also a very good swimmer. And the last one is Raymond Hollington—"

"It's Raymond Dunn," I said.

"How do you know?" Paul asked. Cherry and Denise were also standing there.

"Because he says in his letter he wants to be a teacher, and he said the river was more fun to swim in than the town pool. So he's a swimmer. His name is Raymond Dunn."

Oh my god.

I looked closer at the photograph. He was lean and had short brown hair, neatly combed. His shorts were fabulously short, as they mostly were back in the early 70s. He wore a polo shirt, tucked in, and he was smiling at the camera with a bunch of other guys.

I had to wonder if his boyfriend was one of them.

But my eyes were drawn back to Raymond. He had such a beautiful smile. It was him. I just knew it.

"It's him. His name is Raymond Dunn," I said again.

Cherry was already at her desk, tapping away at the

keyboard. "I can find three Raymond Dunn's listed in New South Wales. Cross-reference with . . ." She tapped away some more and squinted at the screen. "Date of birth . . . 1946; no. 1963; no. 1954; bingo. Raymond Dunn, born 1954. Age eighteen in 1972." She scribbled something down on a piece of paper and handed it to me. "His phone number."

"Holy shit, girl. Honestly, you should contact National Security for a job." I stared at the number, then looked back at her. "Uh, was this information gained legally? Just wondering if I could get into trouble for this."

She smirked. "Yeah of course."

There was a solid twenty per cent chance she was lying.

But we had a phone number.

"What's going on?" Julian's deep voice asked.

I held up the paper. "We have a contact number for a Raymond Dunn. Graduated from Northbury High in 1972."

Julian blinked and a slow smile spread across his handsome face. "Wow."

I handed the paper to him. "You should do the honours. Because I'm likely to have a rambling fit on the phone and he'll block me for harassment. Or call me an ambulance, I don't know. It's just probably best if I don't be involved with the initial contact."

Julian took the piece of paper with Raymond's name and number on it and went into his office. I didn't know if he was hoping for privacy, but we all followed him in. I sat opposite him, Cherry sat next to me, Denise, Paul, and Theo stood behind us.

He dialled the number and we waited. I swear I could hear the clock tick.

After an eternity, the phone picked up. "Hello?" It was a man's voice. He sounded older, but by no means frail.

"Ah yes, hello," Julian replied. "My name is Julian Pollard and I'm calling from the mail distribution centre in Alexandria, Sydney. Am I speaking to a Mr Raymond Dunn?"

"Ah yes, thank you, but I'm not interested, thank you."

"No, Mr Dunn, I'm not selling anything," Julian said quickly. "This isn't . . . Um, the mail distribution centre is the new name for the dead letter office. We found some letters we think may belong to you."

"Letters?"

"Yes. There's a few of them. Would you be familiar with any mail addressed to a Dearest Milton James?"

Everyone held their breath. I held Cherry's hand.

The phone was quiet for a long moment. "Oh my god," came the whispered reply.

"Mr Dunn, are you there?"

"Yes, yes. I just . . . I haven't heard that name in a long time."

Julian smiled at me. "These letters have been here at the distribution centre for a long time, Mr Dunn. We never thought we'd find the man who sent them."

Mr Dunn let out a breathy laugh. God, was he crying? Please don't be crying. I couldn't handle it if he were crying . . .

I put my free hand to my face. "Is he okay?" I whispered.

"Mr Dunn," Julian said. "Are you okay?"

"Oh yes, I'm just . . . I can't believe it. I haven't thought about those letters in . . . well, a very long time."

"If it's okay with you, I'd like to return these letters to you. Do you have a postal address I can forward them to?"

"Yes, of course . . ."

Julian wrote down the address on his notepad, then stared at it as he chewed the inside of his lip. "Actually, Mr Dunn, if it's okay with you, I'd like to personally hand-deliver these. These letters have become legendary in this department. For over forty years." Julian smiled at me. "If it's okay with you, I'd really like to deliver them to you myself."

CHAPTER SEVENTEEN

WE'D FOUND HIM.

We'd found the man who wrote the Dearest Milton James letters.

It took all of us, and there was absolutely no way I could've found this information on my own. Certainly not so quickly.

But it was a good lesson for the benefit of teamwork. Sharing mystery cases, or difficult cases, or seemingly lost causes, just might be doable if we put our skills together.

Julian was going to hand-deliver the letters to Raymond tomorrow, being a Saturday. He didn't say it to the rest of the team, but I was going with him. There was no way I wasn't going.

It didn't feel real, but we were all so happy and hyped for the rest of the afternoon, the remainder of the shift passed in a blur. And before I knew it, Paul and Theo were putting their cages away. I checked the time.

4.58pm.

Holy shit.

I rushed to pack up my stuff.

"Oh, how was your super-hot date last night?" Paul asked as he was packing his desk.

Just so happened that Julian walked out of his office to take his coffee cup to the sink.

"Oh, so hot," I replied, grinning. "And tonight's going to be even hotter."

"Is that why your hair turned orange?" Theo joked. His jokes were so bad.

"Yep, totally the reason."

"I like how the orange matches your boot laces instead of your boots this time," he said.

I glanced to my feet. "Oh, thanks. Colour coordination is important to us gay folks."

"Sooo," Paul hedged. "Second hot date, two nights in a row. It must be serious."

Julian stopped near the breakroom door and turned to face me. By this time, Theo and Cherry were also standing there, waiting for me to answer.

Christ. What was I supposed to say to that?

Julian was right there!

So I decided to put all my freaking cards on the table. "I hope so," I replied, choosing not to look at Julian. "He's amazing, and he's sweet and smart and gorgeous and funny." Then I put my hands about ten inches apart. "And you know those huge salami they hang in the deli windows?"

"Oh, that's enough," Julian said, barrelling into the breakroom.

Cherry laughed.

"Yeah, I get it," Paul said. "No need to go there."

Theo said, "I don't get . . ." Then his gaze went to mine, eyes wide. "Oh."

Yep, he got it.

"Anyway," I said brightly. "I better run if I'm going to catch the bus. Need to make myself all pretty." I laughed as I walked out with Cherry. "He's gonna kill me for that," I told her.

She laughed again. "They don't know who you're talking about though."

And then my phone beeped. It was a message from Julian. I laughed but then I wondered if he'd be mad.

Salami?

I took that as a good sign.

Oh yes, please. A good nine to ten inches tonight, as promised.

His text bubble appeared then disappeared, then appeared and disappeared again. But then my phone rang. It was him. I showed the screen with his name on it to Cherry before I hit Answer.

"Am I in trouble?" I asked instead of saying hello.

"I'm considering it."

"Mm, do I get to pick my punishment?"

He laughed. "No. Then it wouldn't be a punishment."

"I could pretend to not like it. If that helps."

He chuckled again. "I'll pick you up at seven. You might want to bring a bag with clothes for tomorrow if we're going to deliver these letters to Mr Dunn."

Mmm, I was staying another night.

"Need me to bring anything else?"

"No. I have everything." He paused. "And Malachi?"

"Yes?"

"I hope you like salami."

I laughed and the line went dead in my ear. I might have blushed. Cherry took one look at me and shook her head, but the bus pulled up and we couldn't sit together because it was crowded.

I waved to her as I got off and she yelled out, "Good luck!"

I was getting giddy.

This was ridiculous. But so help me, I was so ready for tonight.

I swung past the chemist and grabbed extra condoms and lube and a few douching bulbs and put my time to good use when I got home.

I showered, cleaning my body, inside and out. Dressed in my skin-tight white jeans, a neon orange T-shirt, and a white bomber jacket. My black boots with the orange laces matched my hair perfectly.

Not that it mattered. I had no intention of wearing anything for long.

I put some food out for Buster Jones so he wouldn't be yelling at my balcony door all night, and at five to seven, my phone beeped.

I'm here.

I grabbed my bag and skipped all the way downstairs and to his car like an excited boy on Christmas morning. "Oh, salami home delivered," I said. "I hope you packed the extra-large."

He grinned. "Nine and a half inches, just like you ordered."

I laughed but then . . . "Is it actually nine and a half inches. Because I wouldn't doubt that at all. But have you measured it?"

He laughed again. "Good evening, Malachi."

So that was a yes. "I totally would have measured it too, if it were mine. Let's be real."

He laughed some more. "So, I've ordered dinner to be delivered at eight thirty. I felt like Vietnamese. Is that okay?"

"Perfect. Um . . . any reason we're not eating for an hour and a half?"

He glanced over at me. "So here's what I was thinking . . . I've had an erection problem since we spoke on the phone. It won't go away on its own."

I laughed, my insides warming deliciously. "Oh no. Is that something I can help with?"

"Well, I'd like to think it's your fault," he said with a grin. "I just have to think of you and my body starts to . . . get a mind of its own. Then you mentioned the salami thing and if you were in trouble and could pick your own punishment, and I began picturing what I'm planning on doing to you tonight and how it's going to feel."

"Okay, I like where this is going. What do you plan on doing to me tonight?"

"Well, that's the thing. Round one, intermission with dinner, hence the order for eight thirty, then round two afterwards. How does that sound?"

"That sounds like a three-course meal to me." He chuckled and I slid my hand onto his thigh and up a little higher, and a little higher, until my pinkie traced the crease at his crotch. "Now about that erection."

"I'm not kidding. I have a permanent hard-on. I haven't been like this since I was sixteen."

I just went right ahead and palmed his monster cock, which was slung across to his hip and facing me. "Good. I get the feeling I'll be wanting it a lot."

He moved my hand and shifted in his seat. "Malachi," he said, his voice strained. "If you want round one to last more than thirty seconds, you're gonna need to give me some slack."

I laughed and put my hand on my own leg instead. "Okay, okay."

He shook his head and ended up laughing. "You are trouble."

"I am trouble? Or I'm in trouble?"

"Both."

Aaaaaand twenty minutes later, I was starting to think I was in actual trouble.

I was sprawled naked on his bed, slicked with lube, my arsehole stretched and stretched until I whined at him to stop playing with me.

But then he rolled on a condom and poured on some more lube, and I was beginning to wonder if he'd actually fit.

I leaned up on my elbows. "Holy fuck."

He grinned and turned me over so I was face down on his bed, and he brought my arse up a little. Positioning me just how he wanted me. He spread me, teased and stretched me some more, fingers, tongue, and a lot more lube.

It was at this point I entered another realm of pleasure.

Everything, every touch, every groan was too much and not enough. I was too desperate. I wanted more. I wanted his cock. I wanted to feel him inside me. I want to take him, feel him. I wanted him to own me.

"Julian," I growled. "Give it to me."

"Oh, baby, I will," he whispered. Then his fingers were digging into my hips and the blunt head of his huge cock was at my hole.

This was what I wanted.

"Yes," I breathed, trying to back onto him.

He held me still, spread wide, and he began to push into me. He was slow and gentle, murmuring soft nothings of encouragement and desire. And he pushed a little further . . . The stretch, the burn, it was a lot.

It was too much.

I gripped the sheets. "Oh fuck," I cried out.

Julian froze but didn't pull out. He stayed still and rubbed my back. "Are you okay?"

I took a deep breath and exhaled slowly, and the pain eased. Julian added more lube, then rocked a little and something seemed to give and he slipped in past the tight ring of muscle.

Fuck. Was that just the head?

"Oh god."

But it was easier then, and he pushed in another inch, then another. He groaned like I'd never heard a man groan. He gripped my hips and pulled back a little only to slide in even further.

There was so much of him. "Fuck, Julian, you're so big."

He leaned over my back, pushing in some more, his lips near my ear. "Breathe, Malachi."

"Fuck." I took some rapid-fire breaths and eventually slowed my breathing right down. I relaxed, and my mind went to that other place.

That other place where only pleasure exists.

"That's it, baby. Breathe nice and slow for me," he murmured again, his voice tight. He held himself still. "You can take me, I know you can. You can take all of me." Then he began to push in again, giving me more and more of him, pulling out a little only to push back in.

I dug my forehead into the covers, arching my back, and let him do what he wanted with my arse. He was so far inside me, pushing further in until his fingers dug into my hips. "Fuck. To the hilt. Ugh, Malachi," he groaned, then began to slowly thrust, moaning with each movement.

Or maybe that was me.

There was some noise coming from somewhere in the room . . . I think it might have been me.

But he held me still and rolled his hips, thrusting a little harder. "Oh baby, I can't last like this. Stroke your cock for me."

My cock?

God, I forgot I even had one . . .

And I was surprisingly hard. I hadn't even realised. Yes, it all just felt so good, but I was too caught up in him, too caught up in that feeling of euphoria to think about my dick.

A few long pulls were all it took for fireworks to spark behind my eyes. Was being so full of dick a magic button for me?

I think it was.

I came like a tonne of bricks and Julian slammed into me, groaning long and loud as he filled the condom inside me. I felt every pulse and every jerk of his cock, and every moan vibrated through me.

I'd never felt anything like it.

He slowly, slowly pulled out of me, then collapsed on my back, breathing hard and whispering sweet nothings in my ear. His still-hard cock was pushed between my legs, and so god help me, I wanted more.

Even after all that.

I wiggled my arse a little. "More?"

Julian laughed. "Want dinner first?"

"No."

He stilled. "Are you being serious?"

"I think I'm going to want a lot more. I told you that."

So, without another word, Julian climbed off the bed and dragged me by my ankle so my arse was at the side of the bed. He pulled off the used condom, gave himself a few strokes, and rolled on a new condom. Flipped the lid on the lube, poured it over both of us, positioned my hips over the edge of the bed so my arse was at that perfect height, and he just slid straight back into me.

All the fucking way.

"Oh my god," I whimpered, gripping the rumpled bedding.

He whispered in my ear, his hands on my hips, his cock buried inside me. "I told you I haven't been this horny since I was sixteen. I want to fuck you all night long. I don't know what you've done to me. But I want more."

I melted into a fiery pit of lava, and he did exactly what he said he was going to do.

Except this time, the fireworks behind my eyes were blinding, the pleasure was so encompassing, so thorough, my whole body trembled and convulsed.

He'd found my prostate.

When it was over, when I couldn't take anymore, he cradled me in his arms.

I would never be the same again. I felt put back together and humbled, and a teeny tiny, quite possibly a little bit in love.

We ate the Vietnamese food a little cold but I didn't care one bit. Then he showered me, washed me, tenderness in every touch, and we went back to bed.

To sleep this time, though. He pulled me straight into his arms, his hold on me lovely and secure, infrequent kisses in my hair.

I wanted to tell him thank you. I wanted to tell him he was amazing and that he could call me at any time. No matter where I was in the world, I would come to him, be naked with my arse in the air any time he wanted it.

That was a sign of the perfect top. Well, for me at least.

But two mind-blowing orgasms later, a belly full of food,

and strong arms around me, and all the things I wanted to say floated away when I closed my eyes.

I SLEPT like the dead and I woke to a smiley Julian sliding a tray of toast and coffee onto the bed. "Morning, sleepyhead."

I had to blink a few times. "Hey."

"We have to leave soon," he said. "If you want to come with me to deliver these letters to Mr Dunn."

I sat up, still naked, and pulled the covers up to hide my junk. I sipped my coffee. It was divine. "What time is it?"

"Half eight."

"I've never slept so well."

"I think I wore you out."

"You can wear me out like that any time you want."

He hummed. "Are you sore this morning?"

I wiggled my butt, taking a mental stocktake of any soreness or aches and pains. "Nope. Feel fine." And I did. That was no lie. All that stretching and prepping that I'd complained about at the time had come in clutch. "You know what you're doing. I was in very good hands."

He blushed a little. "I like looking after you."

I picked up a slice of toast. "You did more than that. And you brought me breakfast in bed. I feel like a king."

He grinned. "I'm going to take a shower. Won't be long."

IT DIDN'T REALLY HIT me what we were about to do until we were in the car and driving to the Northern Beaches to go meet Raymond.

We were meeting *the* Dearest Milton James man. We were returning his letters to him after all this time.

Those letters that had sat there for so long . . .

I tried to prepare myself for bad news. It was a possibility. Actually, it was more than likely going to end in some kind of bad news.

That he never saw his lover again.

That they did see each other but couldn't be together, they had to marry girls even though they still loved each other.

Or maybe Raymond would tell us every letter was complete fiction. This whole thing had been a made-up story in hopes of having it read on-air.

I wasn't sure which would be worse.

"Here it is," Julian said, pulling up to the kerb. The house was cute, quaint, and probably worth a fortune, given its location. Raymond had done well for himself, obviously.

I just hoped he was happy.

With a nervous smile and a sinking heart, I got out of the car. Julian was by my side, but I stopped outside the gate. "God, Julian, what if he—"

"Hey," Julian replied gently. "Whatever he says, whatever he does with the letters is fine. There's no wrong reaction, and whatever he says or does is the right answer for him."

I nodded. He was right. He was always right. We had no control over Raymond's reaction. We could just give him back the letters and be on our way without so much as a conversation.

That's it.

Then our job would be done.

With a nod, Julian gave my arm a squeeze, then opened the gate for me. I walked along the small path, up the three porch steps, and with a deep breath, I pressed the doorbell.

A dog barking echoed on the other side of the door, then "Oh, Penelope, shush." Then the door opened and a man stood there. He was around seventy, at a guess, with short, neat grey hair, faded blue eyes, and a kind face. He was holding a Pomeranian, who I guessed was Penelope.

"Raymond Dunn?" I asked.

He smiled cautiously. "Yes?"

I put my hand to my chest. "My name's Malachi Keogh, and this is Julian Pollard. We're from the Dead Letter Office." I knew Julian hated when it was called that. "We called yesterday about some found letters."

His smile widened. "Yes, please come in."

CHAPTER EIGHTEEN

RAYMOND DUNN, or Ray, as he told us, showed us through to his living room, still carrying his little dog under his arm. "Can I get you both anything to drink?"

"No, I'm fine, thank you," I replied.

"No thank you," Julian said.

We sat on the double seater. Ray took the single. The room was full of expensive furniture, gorgeous decorative art pieces, and paintings on the walls. Photographs too. They were pieces from all over the world, as far as I could tell. He'd very clearly lived a full life.

Penelope sat perched on Ray's knee, and while she was cute, I had no delusions about her ability to kill me and dispose of my remains.

Julian took the letters out of his satchel, and still with the twine tied around them, he handed them over to Ray like he was handing over the Holy Grail.

Ray held them and let out a laugh. He got a little teary. "Oh my god." He laughed again. "I can't believe it." He pulled the twine and opened the first letter. Then he looked up at us and put his hand to his mouth. "I cannot believe they survived all this time. How? How are they still intact? You said they sat in your office for forty years? How did you ever trace them to me?"

Julian nodded. "Because they had no deliverable address or returnable address, they found their way to the Dead Letter Office. They were lost for a time, we believe. They were found down the back of a pigeon hole or a cabinet where they must have spent twenty years. Then the Dead Letter Office moved to a new warehouse, and when everything was stripped out, they were found. Someone had the good sense to keep them aside and not have them thrown to archives or destroyed." Julian shrugged. "They'd been in my office for as long as anyone knows. I was told people had tried to find their home but had no luck."

Ray was reading the letters and nodding. He was still teary-eyed but happy, amazed even. "Oh my god, I remember this. I wrote about Deidre being annoying," he laughed, but then he turned sad. "My little sister. She died in 1992."

Oh no.

"I'm so sorry," I whispered.

He smiled gratefully. "No, it's fine. I'd forgotten about this. She followed us around all day. We went swimming. It was a forgotten memory, so thank you."

He skimmed over another page, shaking his head in wonder. "How did you know it was me?"

"Well," I began, "we pieced together all the clues. There was a mention of the hardware store owner, and most archived business registrations are online now. Honestly, without the internet, we'd have gotten nowhere. But finding the hardware store registration gave us Northbury as the town." I smiled at him. "The other people in our team all did their bit. Cherry found the town. Denise found out about the radio show called *Dearest Milton James*. Theo sourced out the high school yearbooks for Northbury High and we found a few Raymonds, given we didn't really know what year you graduated, so it was a process of elimination. And Paul followed the leads on the mentions of Duntroon."

And there it was. The mention of Duntroon, of the army, of the war.

Julian spoke next. "We could find four men from the Milldale council area who were enlisted through conscription. But at the end of the day, we had no right to find that person. We could find you, the author of the letters, yes. But given you'd used an alias for the man you wrote to, we decided to honour that and keep his identity a secret too."

I slid my hand over Julian's and squeezed, giving him a smile. "Julian decided that, and he was right."

Ray looked at us then, realising that, yes, I was holding Julian's hand. He nodded and went back to his letters. "I really appreciate that."

I had to know . . .

"Mr Dunn, is he . . . ? Is the man you wrote to . . . did you ever see him again?"

"Malachi," Julian cautioned.

"Sorry," I added quickly. "I just . . . I know it's not my business, but these letters just mean so much. They're just beautiful, and my little romantic heart just has to know. Did you go to university? Or did you take the job at the council with your aunt? Did you see him again?"

Ray laughed again, holding a letter to his chest. "Oh, you remind me of me. Well, a much younger me, that is. Yes, I went to university. I became an English teacher, and I taught high school English and drama for over forty-five years. Loved even the worst day." He sighed. "I've been retired now for seven years."

"That's amazing," I said. "I'm so happy to hear that."

"And Steve," he said wistfully. "Seems like a lifetime ago. I guess it was . . ."

Steve?

Steve wasn't one of the two names we had.

But there was a Steven. The army guy whose record had no details. It had all been redacted, apparently.

"His name was Steve?" I asked. "Steven?"

Ray tilted his head, then he laughed. "Not was, is. Steve's still alive. Well, I think he is. He left to get some milk and he's not home yet. But the frigates have been going up and down the coast this week and he's probably watching them. You see, he spent forty-eight years in the army. And you can take a man out of the military but you can't take the military out of the man." He sighed, smiling fondly. "Of course the military knew about us, but they just pretended they didn't. It was probably because he knew too much by then, they could never fire him."

"Wait . . . he left to get milk?" I asked. "You . . . you and Steve . . . the man you wrote to in these letters . . . you live with him?"

Ray was positively gleeful. "Oh yes. We've been together since 1972. Married in 1992. We had a civil ceremony in Denmark. Not that it meant much back here in Australia, but it was real for us. We had our second wedding here in 2018."

I could have honestly cried.

Damn tears.

"I'm not going to cry," I said, and Julian laughed and let go of my hand to rub my back. "I'm sorry, I thought for sure something bad had happened. The letters stopped after he went to Duntroon, so of course my mind thought something terrible. I'm so relieved."

Ray laughed. "He left for Duntroon, and I left for university not long after. When we knew he wasn't leaving the country, we wrote to each other, keeping our letters very coded, as you could imagine. He went straight into administration, thankfully. And within a year he was moved to Holsworthy and into defence intelligence."

Well, that would explain why everything was redacted.

Ray smiled at some far-off memory. "Holsworthy was much closer to my university. He would come visit every chance he got." Penelope jumped down and ran to the door, barking excitedly now. "Steve's home now," Raymond said.

We heard the door open and a deep voice murmuring to, I assumed, the dog. And in walked a tall man, thick-set, his dark grey hair short and neat, a strong jaw and heavy eyebrows. He had a bottle of milk in one hand, Penelope in his other arm. He might have been seventy-something years old but he looked like he could snap me with one harsh word.

Julian and I both stood, and Ray joined us. "Steve, my love, come in. I want you to meet this lovely couple from the letter office."

Couple?

He thought we were a couple.

I didn't correct him, and neither did Julian.

Steve eyed us like we were in an interrogation room. "Oh stop, you're scaring them," Ray said with a laugh. He introduced us by name, and we shook his hand, and yes, his grip was like a raptor talon.

I didn't know whether to cry or salute him.

Ray then exchanged the milk and Penelope for the pile of letters. "Here are the letters I told you about." Raymond had Steve sit in the chair and smiled at us. "I still cannot believe they had them after all these years."

Julian and I sat back down, more straight-backed than before. I was relieved Mr Military had the same effect on Julian that he had on me.

Steve watched us for a scrutinising second, maybe looking at how close we were sitting, probably trying to determine if we were a couple and, by association, how much he would divulge of his personal life in front of strangers. After he came to some mental conclusion, he looked at the envelope first. "Dearest Milton James." He shook his head. "Haven't heard that name in a long time." Then he opened the first letter. "Your handwriting hasn't changed, love."

And my heart just melted a little bit.

Ray sat on the armrest and kept his hand on Steve's shoulder. He read over two letters, skimmed a third, then folded it neatly and put it back in the envelope. He didn't open the fourth.

Julian patted my knee. "We should get going. Thank you for being so welcoming. I'm so pleased we could finally deliver the letters to their rightful owner. It's been an honour, actually, to finally meet you both."

He stood up and I followed suit. I could have probably stayed and listened to their love story all day, but it was pretty obvious that Steve was a little emotional.

We owed it to them both to be able to read these letters in private.

"Thank you, both," I said. "For being the happy ever after these letters deserve. I'll remember them forever."

"Aww." Ray stood up and gave me a quick hug. I wasn't expecting it but it was sweet. He pulled away and looked at us both. "You remind me of a certain young couple in these letters." Then he pointed his thumb at Steve. "He used to call me his little Ray of sunshine, you know."

Steve frowned at him. "I still call you that."

Ray rolled his eyes, and I nudged Julian. "I'm the ray of sunshine, by the way."

Julian tried not to smile. "We know."

I grinned at Ray. "Thank you."

He put his hand on my forearm. "No, thank *you*."

We said our final goodbyes and I walked down the steps, along the path and out the gate, all without crying. But then I got halfway to the car and the tears came.

Julian saw, and with a frown, he pulled me in for a hug. "You okay?"

I nodded against him. "Happy tears. I'm so happy."

Which was so obvious, given I was sobbing in his arms.

"A perfect ending, right?"

I nodded again. "So perfect. They've been together for fifty years. I thought for sure he was going to say he'd died, but nope, he was getting milk and looking at ships on the ocean."

It was so freaking adorable, I cried harder.

Julian laughed and rubbed my back, kissing the side of my head. "Did you want to get some fish and chips while we're on the Northern Beaches? We can sit and watch the ships on the ocean."

I pulled back and wiped at my face. "That would be perfect. Sorry for crying."

He lifted my chin and kissed me sweetly. "Don't ever apologise for having a heart, Malachi."

EPILOGUE

FOUR YEARS LATER

I WALKED into the breakroom with a birthday cake in the shape of a cat, and I slid it onto the table underneath the shrine to Glenda. "Happy birthday, Glenda!" I said.

"Yay, cake!" Denise cried, quickly grabbing some plates from the cupboard.

"And I'm not eating the cat's arse this year," I warned. "I've had it every year since I started. It's somebody else's turn."

Cherry smiled as she took some cutlery from the drawer. "I'll have the arse this year."

I nudged her hip with mine as I unrolled some paper towel. "Yes, wifey, you get that arse."

Cherry and I called each other wifey all the time. It started as work-wife and got shortened over the years.

Julian walked in and pretended not to have heard me. Not much that came out of my mouth surprised him anymore. It didn't surprise anyone anymore.

Yes, I'd been at my job for over four years. A record that my father was very proud of. And yes, Julian and I would celebrate our four-year anniversary in a few weeks. And we'd been living together for three years. Was it a lot to be living and working together? Maybe for other people, but not us. We'd been inseparable since day one, basically. We spent every day and night together when we lived apart, it just made sense that we move in together. His townhouse was more than big enough, and my rent helped him pay his ridiculous mortgage.

And it meant we got to have scorching hot sex all the time. Like *all* the time. We had so much sex, that my best friend Moni began to send me pictures of broken arseholes. She stopped when I started sending her 'thank you, that was delicious' memes.

I didn't actually think they were delicious, but I told her my anatomy could handle his anatomy just fine. More than fine, actually, especially with how he looked after me. She was just concerned about my booty, which I appreciated, but she loved Julian and knew he'd never hurt me.

Julian made me a coffee while I cut up some cake, and then we sang happy birthday to Glenda. It was a ritual every year, and no, I never knew her but it stopped being weird a long time ago.

I just went with it now.

As we were eating our cake, Theo was telling us all about his new garden composting system, which was kinda gross but he was excited, and a happy Theo was hard not to like. He did date the Milldale librarian for a short time, but that fizzled out and he'd now been seeing a nice lady called Yvonne for almost a year. They met at a model train convention, so the composting was a nice subject change from toy trains. If you could believe that.

Ignoring Theo, Paul pointed to his newspaper. "Hey,

Malachi, your Dearest Milton James couple are in the paper."

I stared at him. "Is it the obituaries? Because oh my god, Paul, it better not be."

"No, they're not dead," he said, looking at me like I was the weird one. "They gave the letters to the Australian War Museum. It's a whole page write-up."

"Oh my . . . let me see," I whispered, turning the paper around so we could all read it.

And there was a photograph of Ray and Steve in their home, looking as spritely as they had four years ago. They stood together, grinning at the camera, a close-up of the letters on the table in front of them, still with the twine tied around them, the words Dearest Milton James on top.

They gave the letters to the museum, marking a significant contribution because of the LGBTQ content. They were proud to be able to share the letters, showcasing the need to hide who they were all those years ago. Something they didn't need to do anymore.

It briefly touched on Steve's time in the defence force, though it didn't mention anything about intelligence, his level of security clearance, or his redacted file. It mostly focused on Ray, as he was the author.

I read the last part out loud. "'The letters were saved by the Dead Letter Office, Ray says.'"

"The mail distribution centre," Julian corrected quietly. He was such a dork.

I continued to read it out loud. "'They'd sat in storage for almost four decades until a nice couple who work at the office decided to try and find the rightful owner.'"

"Awww," Denise said. "He called you a nice couple."

"We *are* a nice couple," I replied.

"Well, Julian's nice," Cherry said. I gasped, offended.

She rolled her eyes. "Malachi, I've heard the judgemental commentary you give on *Drag Race* after a few wines. Nice is not the word I'd use."

I took a deep breath and rose above a snarky reply. "I'll be putting out expressions of interest for a new work-wife. Please stay tuned."

Cherry just laughed, but then she turned back to the newspaper. "It's a nice write-up. We should put it on the board underneath Glenda."

"Ooh, great idea." The whole article was lovely and the photo of them made me all gooey. "They're still adorable. Look at them."

Paul took the page from his newspaper and stuck it to the wall underneath Glenda's shrine. Everyone took a moment to appreciate it but went back to their coffees and more cake.

Except Julian and me . We stood there and looked at the photo a little longer. Julian put his arm around me and kissed the side of my head. It was rare for us to display any kind of affection at work—we just didn't do that—but this was warranted.

"That'll be us one day," he murmured. "Fifty years from now."

I would never tire of hearing him say stuff like that. "Yes, it will," I replied. I had no doubt. We were absolutely perfect for each other, in every way.

I nodded to the photo. "I'll be the cute one."

Julian laughed. "Yes, you will be. And I'll be the one who looks after the cute one."

"Yes, you will."

He sighed and kissed the side of my head again. "For-ever, Malachi."

"Hmm, my second favourite F-word."

He laughed. "Get to work."

I grinned. "Yes, boss."

THE END

ABOUT THE AUTHOR

N.R. Walker is an Australian author, who loves her genre of gay romance. She loves writing and spends far too much time doing it, but wouldn't have it any other way.

She is many things: a mother, a wife, a sister, a writer. She has pretty, pretty boys who live in her head, who don't let her sleep at night unless she gives them life with words.

She likes it when they do dirty, dirty things... but likes it even more when they fall in love.

She used to think having people in her head talking to her was weird, until one day she happened across other writers who told her it was normal.

She's been writing ever since...

ALSO BY N.R. WALKER

Cronin's Key IV - Kennard's Story

Exchange of Hearts

The Spencer Cohen Series, Book One

The Spencer Cohen Series, Book Two

The Spencer Cohen Series, Book Three

The Spencer Cohen Series, Yanni's Story

Blood & Milk

The Weight Of It All

A Very Henry Christmas (The Weight of It All 1.5)

Perfect Catch

Switched

Imago

Imagines

Imagoes

Red Dirt Heart Imago

On Davis Row

Finders Keepers

Evolved

Galaxies and Oceans

Private Charter

Nova Praetorian

A Soldier's Wish

Upside Down

The Hate You Drink

Sir

Tallowwood

Reindeer Games

The Dichotomy of Angels

Throwing Hearts

Pieces of You - Missing Pieces #1

Pieces of Me - Missing Pieces #2

Pieces of Us - Missing Pieces #3

Lacuna

Tic-Tac-Mistletoe

Bossy

Code Red

Titles in Audio:

Cronin's Key

Cronin's Key II

Cronin's Key III

Red Dirt Heart

Red Dirt Heart 2

Red Dirt Heart 3

Red Dirt Heart 4

The Weight Of It All

Switched

Point of No Return

Breaking Point

Starting Point

Spencer Cohen Book One

Tic-Tac-Mistletoe

Lacuna

Bossy

Code Red

Free Reads:

Sixty Five Hours

Learning to Feel

His Grandfather's Watch (And The Story of Billy and Hale)

The Twelfth of Never (Blind Faith 3.5)

Twelve Days of Christmas (Sixty Five Hours Christmas)

Best of Both Worlds

Translated Titles:

Italian

Fiducia Cieca (Blind Faith)

Attraverso Questi Occhi (Through These Eyes)

Preso alla Sprovvista (Blindside)

Il giorno del Mai (Blind Faith 3.5)

Cuore di Terra Rossa Serie (Red Dirt Heart Series)

Natale di terra rossa (Red dirt Christmas)

Intervento di Retrofit (Elements of Retrofit)

A Chiare Linee (Clarity of Lines)

Senso D'appartenenza (Sense of Place)

Spencer Cohen Serie (including Yanni's Story)

Punto di non Ritorno (Point of No Return)

Punto di Rottura (Breaking Point)

Punto di Partenza (Starting Point)

Imago (Imago)

Il desiderio di un soldato (A Soldier's Wish)

Scambiato (Switched)

Galassie e Oceani (Galaxies and Oceans)

French

Confiance Aveugle (Blind Faith)

A travers ces yeux: Confiance Aveugle 2 (Through These Eyes)

Aveugle: Confiance Aveugle 3 (Blindside)

À Jamais (Blind Faith 3.5)

Cronin's Key Series

Au Coeur de Sutton Station (Red Dirt Heart)

Partir ou rester (Red Dirt Heart 2)

Faire Face (Red Dirt Heart 3)

Trouver sa Place (Red Dirt Heart 4)

Le Poids de Sentiments (The Weight of It All)

Un Noël à la sauce Henry (A Very Henry Christmas)

Une vie à Refaire (Switched)

Evolution (Evolved)

Galaxies & Océans

German

Flammende Erde (Red Dirt Heart)

Lodernde Erde (Red Dirt Heart 2)

Sengende Erde (Red Dirt Heart 3)

Ungezähmte Erde (Red Dirt Heart 4)

Vier Pfoten und ein bisschen Zufall (Finders Keepers)

Ein Kleines bisschen Versuchung (The Weight of It All)

Ein Kleines Bisschen Fur Immer (A Very Henry Christmas)

Weil Leibe uns immer Bliebt (Switched)

Drei Herzen eine Leibe (Three's Company)

Über uns die Sterne, zwischen uns die Liebe (Galaxies and Oceans)

Unnahbares Herz (Blind Faith 1)

Sehendes Herz (Blind Faith 2)

Thai

Sixty Five Hours (Thai translation)

Finders Keepers (Thai translation)

Spanish

Sesenta y Cinco Horas (Sixty Five Hours)

Chinese

Blind Faith